Killer's Crypt

(A DI Shona McKenzie Mystery)

Wendy H. Jones

To Ella

best wishes

Wendy H. Jones

Published by Scott and Lawson

Copyright © Wendy H. Jones, 2017

www.wendyhjones.com

Cover Design by Cathy Helms of Avalon Graphics LLC

ISBN: 978-0-9956457-2-1

DEDICATION

To Caroline Wilkes and Jacky Jones who have stuck by me through thick and thin since our schooldays. Friendships like this don't come along often.

ACKNOWLEDGMENTS

I would like to thank the following people who have helped me in so many ways. Caroline Wilkes for her tireless work with editing. Karen Wilson of Ginger Snap Images, Dundee for the professional author photographs. Nathan Gevers for all his hard work and enthusiasm building the website for my books. Police Scotland for their patience in answering myriad questions about the nuts and bolts of policing. Particular thanks must go to my local police sergeant who has never failed to answer any of my questions with good humour and has supported me in my endeavour.

.

1

A dark shroud of fog cloaked the area in eerie stillness. Icy tendrils, at once caressing, then, without warning, smothering. The feeble light of a small torch consumed in its deadly, yawning, chasm. The blonde-haired woman clung tightly to the hand of her companion. His stride sure, hers less so. She tripped. He pulled her up. His laughter sank into the enveloping fog, no match for its deadly pull.

"Mind out, now. We don't want you breaking your beautiful neck."

"Did we *really* have to come here? I loathe hills." She paused. The slow grinding of the cogs in her head could almost be heard. "And walking. My shoes'll be ruined."

"It will be worth it, my beauty, it will be worth it."

"There's water running down my neck."

The tall man shrugged off his jacket, wrapped it round her shoulders. Pulled her close.

"I'll protect you. No harm will become you."

Oblivious to the freezing fog, his strong grip pulled her forward. Up the steep mountain path. She stumbled but he held her. Yanked her gently upright.

"Oww. Let's go home. This is horrible."

"Not long now."

As if conjured up by his voice, a small bothy appeared, ghost like, in the fog. They dashed through the door into the warmth within. A burning coal fire provided the only light.

He gently removed his jacket from her shoulders. Hung it on the back of a rustic wooden chair. The designer folds dropped perfectly.

The young woman threw herself onto a tartan, overstuffed sofa. Sank into its embrace. Sighed. Bending over, she gazed at her shoes as though they offended her. "They're ruined."

"I needed to bring you here for a reason. There's something I need to do. I will buy you more shoes." He pulled her up from the seat.

Her bright smile lit her face. All thoughts of cold and fog forgotten. It's time, she thought.

He knew it was time. But this night would not play out the way she imagined.

His rough hands embraced her soft cheeks. He cupped her face and gently kissed her. A moan escaped from her ruby-red lipsticked lips. Chosen, with care, to match the colour of her shoes.

One strong twist. Her pretty, little neck snapped. Her body collapsed, only his hands held her upright. He released his grasp. A thud as she dropped to the wooden floor. The light faded from her eyes, in this, the perfect spot. Not for love but for murder.

2

"Outfit by Prada, teeth by Harley Street. I'd hazard a guess she's not a native of this bothy." Detective Inspector Shona McKenzie stared at the dead woman lying at her feet. The pearly whites could dazzle a blind man at a million paces.

"Shoes by Dolce and Gabbana. I'd say your hazarding and guessing are right." Detective Sergeant Nina Chakrabarti knew shoes. This was evidenced by the ice blue Christian Louboutin's which graced her own size sevens. "Funny choice of footwear for a climb up a mountain."

"Says she who prays to the God of designers."

"Roy McGregor, I swear I'm going to add your very dead body to the pile. Then I'll kick it with my designer footwear."

"Nah. You'd miss me too much. Especially when it comes to the canteen run." He chewed on his lip. "No way you'd desecrate a body, even mine."

"Don't tempt me."

"If you pair are finished with the witty repartee, we've a designer corpse which deserves our *full* attention."

"If you pair are waxing lyrical about her claes, I take it our woman here comes from a more upper class family than your average?" Detective Sergeant Peter Johnson sported an egg stained tie, a crumpled suit, and a false English accent towards the end of his sentence. His ironed shirt was, to him, the height of sartorial elegance.

"I'd say so. Those teeth alone must have cost about twenty thousand pounds."

A low whistle came from the doorway where a lanky man was leaning against the doorway.

"You might want to join us, Soldier Boy. Dead bodies need the whole team in attendance. DC's lounging jauntily, whilst the rest of us work, isn't the order of the day."

"Got it, Ma'am." Jason Roberts straightened up and strolled towards them. His stint in the Army proved useful when it came to obeying orders. Sometimes.

Donning blue gloves, Shona pulled the lips back further from the teeth. "A perfect set of designer gnashers. Shouldn't take long to get her dental records and an identity."

"She's a bonny wee thing, so she is. And I'd be liking to get a bit closer."

Five pairs of eyes swivelled towards the Irish accent. A nondescript man with sandy brown hair and a gleam in his eyes, walked towards them.

"Who, might I ask, are you? More to the point why are you strolling around my crime scene like you own the place?"

The fact he'd got through the police cordon should have alerted Shona to his legitimacy. She never let the facts get in the way of a good argument. Not when it came to a crime scene.

"Because, until I certify your bonny wee corpse dead, you can't do much in this crime scene you're holding on to so tightly." He thrust an ID towards Shona.

Shona read it thoroughly then scrutinised the interloper.

"It's not forged. I really am Seamus Harrison, police surgeon of this parish."

"Where's Whitney the whirlwind?"

"I'd be saying whirlwinding down in County Cork.

We're on an exchange for a month. Wasn't expecting a shout out quite so quickly."

"I can vouch for him."
The voice made Shona go weak at the knees. She told her knees to get a grip and strengthen themselves. "Douglas, what an unexpected pleasure. Why does no one tell me what's going on? I mean, I'm only the Detective Inspector in charge of all this."
The man's laugh could probably be heard in County Cork. "Stop being such a fraud. You knew I'd be here." His eyes narrowed but kept their cheery glint. "And I wasn't aware you oversaw the employment of police surgeons."
"My we're tetchy this morning. Kids keep you up, did they?"
The voice belonged to Douglas Lawson, procurator fiscal. Since returning to Scotland three years previously, Shona realised more and more the importance of the procurator fiscal. He was responsible for investigating all sudden and suspicious deaths in Scotland, amongst many other things. They often turned up at the scene of a crime to get an initial view of the situation. The one in Dundee was conscientious to a fault, so he turned up at all the crime scenes. This also had a lot to do with the fact he was Shona's boyfriend. Most of their dates took place whilst viewing a dead body.

Douglas turned and held his hand out to Seamus. "Welcome. You'll be seeing a lot of Shona. Her work day is usually liberally sprinkled with dead bodies." Manly chuckles accompanied a firm handshake.
Shona's face could freeze alcohol. "Boys, when you've finished your male bonding session maybe you could certify this young woman. Take your time

though. I'd hate to break up your mutual admiration society."

"Right you are. Let me be examining our colleen and I'll be out of your hair in no time."

Seamus was quick and methodical, leaving no doubt he was what he said he was. A police surgeon and a damned good one. His confident hands performed tasks proficiently and with great dexterity. He might appear non-descript but when it came to his job he was the exact opposite.

"I'd say your lass has been dead for a few days. Initial cause of death, broken neck. You'll not be surprised, I don't think she died accidently."

"Funny. Why did I know that would be the case? Ah well, thank you, Seamus."

"I take it you'll be collecting bodies from every corner of Scotland again, Shona?" Only Douglas got away with this sort of insolent familiarity. Anyone else would be joining the corpse.

"I jolly well hope not." Her eyes said otherwise.

"I'm sure another will follow before you've had time to eat a bacon roll."

"Any bodies interfering with bacon roll duty will have to wait."

"Maybe not the best thing to be saying to the procurator fiscal." The bothy rocked to the sound of Douglas's laughter. "I'm taking Seamus here for a full Scottish. See if it beats a full Irish."

The men hurried down the hill, arguing amicably about the relative merits of a regional full cooked breakfast.

Shona took one glance at Peter's face. "Don't even think about moaning. Going by your shirt I'd say you've had breakfast already."

"I did, and all healthy. Not a calorie to be found."

"Glad to hear it. I have to say, you're looking the bizz. Shouldn't you be on light duties or something, though?"

Slim, toned and with a healthy tan, he was the fittest he'd been since Shona's arrival.

"Not a bit o' it. Cleared for everything. Lost five stone and the wife's forced me to do all those bloo... blasted exercises. How do the doctors expect a body to get oot of his sick bed and go running?"

Peter's first day back. A stint in coronary care, eight-weeks recovery and another month convalescing, kept him busy and away from his desk. It hadn't dampened his ability to moan.

"Enough with the talk of food. Work, all of you." Shona took a determined step closer to the corpse.

"You pair can haud your horses. I've Annie primed for grilled bacon on wholemeal."

Shona shrugged her shoulders. At least it was healthy. *Am I my brother's keeper?* "Kit on. Remember, no contaminating the evidence.."

Iain Barrow, the team's resident crime scene expert appeared, suited and eager to crack on. His top of the range camera needed a tight grip, and his steady legs, to stop it toppling him over. Dropped it would cause irreparable damage to the floor and possible evidence. He used it with the care and skill only a pro could exhibit, treading with care to avoid contaminating any evidence. Shona thought it was almost trance-like watching him work. Almost. Whilst apparently quietly waiting, her eyes flickered over every detail taking it all in. The woman looked crumpled. Discarded. *What a way to end your life. What brought her to this wild spot?*

Next came casts of footprints, both inside and outside

the bothy. The team joined in. Their work methodical, they catalogued everything. It was hot and difficult work in the confined space. Masks filled with sweat the minute they were put on. They took turns at going outside and breathing fresh air. Too many people in the bothy could destroy evidence. The dead body lay in the middle, in sharp contrast to the buzz going on around her.

Shona bent down and looked at her. A bonny lass, even without the expensive dental work. *She's someone's wee girl. A sibling? A mother? What's your story?* "Who did this to you?"

A miniscule red clutch bag lay next to the body. Shona picked it up and looked inside. Nothing. Not even a lipstick. Either their victim travelled light or the contents disappeared with her killer. Shona searched the girl's pockets, or pocket to be precise. A crumpled ten-pound note, but no ID.

The young woman didn't look like she'd been moved post mortem. It was almost as if the killer had fled without finishing up. Why the hurry? In this remote spot there was no one to disturb him. Or her.

Standing up, Shona groaned and rubbed her back.

"Who found the body?"

"Not sure, Ma'am. POLSA's the bloke with the knowledge." Roy glanced up then returned to his task.

"Peter, you're with me."

Peter leapt up with less groaning and back rubbing.

"Let's interview our witness."

The Police Official Licensed Search Advisor, or POLSA for short, informed them their witness was currently sitting in a police van.

"Oor man a suspect then?"

"Far from it. You'll see."

3

Shona trudged towards the van, Peter in hot pursuit.

"Why all the flaming mystery? You'd think he could just tell us."

She yanked the back door of the van. It flew back and clattered off the back of the vehicle.

"Mind the bodywork, Ma'am. We're getting grief for the cost of vehicle repairs. They could hire another 100 coppers with the amount it costs."

Shona ignored him. She was too busy greeting the van's occupant. The man was sitting in the only chair, calmly swigging from a travel mug.

"Jock, are you our witness?" She couldn't keep the surprise from her voice.

"Aye, Shona, I am."

Despite the rank smell emanating from both his body and the van interior, she leapt inside the vehicle. Jock, a familiar and well-loved figure in Dundee, was a tramp. Before she reached him, an enormous mutt, tail wagging fit to rock the van, launched itself at her.

She battered off the wall and shoved her hands out. "Fagin, down."

The dog ignored her and continued to wash her face, not stopping until strong hands pulled him back. Despite advancing age, Jock still had a soldier's strength. He didn't get to the rank of Sergeant Major by allowing subordinates their own way.

"Sit down, you stupid dug," he commanded.

Fagin obeyed but continued to use his tail to sweep the floor of the van. Its contents were scattered and some flew out the door. A young copper scrabbled about finding them.

"Ma'am, —"

"The dog stays. Unless you fancy taking it for a long walk, that is." Derren Browne could take tips on mind reading from Shona.

"You're fine, Ma'am. The sergeant would shoot me if I abandoned my post."

Shona nodded. "I thought you might agree."

Pulling out a recording device, Shona turned back to her old pal.

"I've a few questions to ask, Jock."

"Aye."

"What brought you up here? A bit far from your usual stomping ground." *And your flat. I wonder how many nights you've spent there since we set it up for you.*

"Me and my wee companion were getting cabin fever. Needed to get out and feel the wind in our hair."

"When did you find her?"

"About six o'clock this morning. I knew I could brew a wee cuppie in here."

"It's called breaking and entering Jock."

"Entering but no' breaking. The door's always open."

"Yeh, right."

"It is, Ma'am." Peter butted in. "The laird lets anyone use it. Everybody takes care o' it."

"Scotland never ceases to amaze me. How trusting." She swivelled back to Jock. "Did you touch anything?"

"No chance. I turned and legged it back to the road. Flagged down a passing car and the driver rang you lot. Came back here to wait for you to turn up."

"Did anything seem out of place to you?"

"Cannae say. Folks leave things and others pick them up. It's well known round these parts."

She glanced at Peter who had an enigmatic look about his chops. *He's hiding something.* Her mind scribbled a note to speak to him the minute they were alone.

"Jock, talk us through your thoughts."

"I've loads of them. None to do with this debacle."

Shona clenched her fists. A reminder to stay patient.

"Why don't we take you back to the station for a feed? I'll talk to you later."

Jock's eyes brightened. Shona could swear Fagin smiled.

She cleared it with the POLSA who readily agreed. "Brian Gevers can take him."

"Brian's one of your best guys. Don't you need him?"

"He's likely to come straight back. Some of the others might do a wee disappearing act to the pub."

"Good plan. You're a wise man, Sergeant."

"Aye. My wisdom needs to whip a few of the young uns into shape."

4

"Peter Johnston. Stop right there."

Peter didn't break step.

"If you need hearing aids then your time in CID is about to come to a grinding halt."

He stopped, and swivelled so fast he overbalanced.

Shona let him struggle up. "Serves you right. What's with the leaving and picking up?"

"What do you mean, Ma'am?"

"I've no time for this. Spit it out or I swear you're on desk duty for the rest of your natural."

He shrugged. "Some of the bothies are used to drop off illegal booze and fags."

"And you didn't think this was important enough to tell me? Are you smoking illegal baccy?"

"I'm no' smoking any baccy. Had to give it up along wi' pies and beer."

"Peter! Are you angling for early retirement?"

"Okay. Okay. I've no recent intel says this one was used for anything. That's why I never told you." He paused and took in Shona's face. Deciding it could splinter glass he carried on. "Jock seems to know more though. I'll have a word with him."

"Good plan."

In their absence, the others searched up hill and down dale. Literally. They'd taken off their hoods and gloves and were standing behind the crime scene tape.
Roy wiped his brow, then dried his hands on his coverall.

The sweat from Iain's hands dripped down the camera.

"Nine thirty and it's already scorching the heather," said Abigail Lau. Her soft highland lilt, held a hint of laughter, mirrored in her slanting Asian eyes. Every man who came into her orbit found themselves in thrall to the Chinese imp. Women too. Abigail was equal opportunities in every sense, including her choice of date.

Shona slapped her sergeant on the shoulder, "Nice of you to join us."

"I got lost. Horribly."

Some months ago, Abigail joined them from the Isle of Skye. The team carted her to and fro until three weeks ago when she bought a car. It became quickly apparent Abigail was at the end of a very long queue when it came to dishing out directional ability.

"Where this time?"

"Brechin."

Shona's laugh could be heard in Brechin itself. "You're right. Horribly. Now you're on task, got an update?"

"We've pretty much covered every inch. Despite last night's fog the area's desert dry."

"Scottish weather never ceases to amaze me. Fog overnight and sunscreen factor fifty during the day."

"Us Scots like to be different."

"You're certainly that.' Despite being born in Scotland, Shona was raised in England making her a tad confused about her origins. "You stay with Roy and wait for the body to be taken away. Keep Iain as well. I want plenty photos taken of the underneath of the body."

Roy groaned. "Those freaking overalls are going to kill me."

"Go commando under them, you wee wuss."

"You might want to strip off every two minutes, Soldier Boy. The rest of us live in the real world."

"Boys. I've several horrible tasks waiting for you back at the salt mines. They should keep you too busy to argue."

The Gulags of Bell Street, otherwise known as HQ, loomed in front of her as she turned into the road. It wasn't strictly HQ any longer, but old habits die hard. Shona had better things to worry her than the name of the station. A briefing with the Chief Inspector lay in her future. The thought of this made her toes curl.

"Of course not, Sir." Shona responded to the chief's suggestion that she might, in some way, be involved with the demise of the young woman in the hills. Her tone remained mild as this was a regular occurrence.

"It seems to me we had none of these goings on prior to your arrival."

"I appreciate that, Sir. I agree it does seem strange." *What happened to Dundee being the murder capital of Scotland? It was called that long before I arrived you silly old goat.*

"Keep me posted, McKenzie." His bowed head signalled her dismissal.

"Sir." She turned and departed, her mind making a note to search out the furthest flung bothy in which to dump his very dead body. She'd heard there were some Brochs in the Shetlands that could do with a wee bit of decoration. The tourists would love it.

5

The path to Shona's office veered towards the coffee machine. Pulling out a grinder, she flipped open the lid and tipped in some Ethiopian beans. A new blend she was trying out to widen her tastes, and support impoverished growers. Coffee was a serious business around these parts. Not a jar of instant to be seen.

She sank into her state of the art leather chair. Leaning over the pristine desk she fired up her computer. She flicked away of speck of dust from the table. Mo had obviously not quite recovered from her husband's death. Her first task was to buy a sat nav. It was worth eighty quid to make sure her team were all present and correct. Abigail would receive a present on her return. If she returned. The matter was debatable, as she might find herself in Cornwall rather than Dundee.

Once the item was purchased and winging its way to her office, she opened up HOLMES. Policing, even in a MIT or Major Incident Team consisted of 40% action, 60% paperwork. She leaned on the generous side towards action with this statement.

HOLMES, or the Home Office Large or Major Enquiry System, was the lifeblood of all police forces, Scottish and English. Assisting them in solving major cases, especially serial killers, it required immediate and constant updating in order to work. This could be difficult when in the middle of a case. Ordinarily Shona would grab someone to do this, but it never hurt to keep her hand in. And she'd be ahead of the game.

The others returned with a clatter and chatter.

Roy popped his head around her door. "We're grabbing breakfast and then I'll get on to HOLMES."

"Already done."

"What! Isn't that a bit below your pay grade?"

"You'll be going down a pay grade if you don't hurry up. Twenty minutes and I want the lot of you in the briefing room. I've already eaten."

As he left, Roy pulled out his mobile and dialled. "Annie, ten bacon rolls. Peter..." His voice faded.

Shona knew the blessed Saint Annie would oblige.

The newly decorated walls of the briefing room were now made of whiteboard. New pens in a variety of colours lay in strategically placed containers. Equally colourful magnets accompanied them.

"Jeez, I knew they were decorating but this is something else." Jason's gaze took in his surroundings.

"Wit on earth?" A couple of deep breaths. "All this fancy change isnae good for a man's heart."

"The high heid yin's always telling us we're broke. How did he pull off this little stunt?"

"Roy, that's enough. Talk about the chief like that again and your head will be presented to him on a platter."

Roy at least had the grace to look slightly ashamed. There was still a smirk tugging at his lips.

Shona continued. "Police Scotland secured some European funding. Something to do with an exchange of ideas, resources and personnel."

"Personnel? Does that mean we get to go to Europe? I bagsie Paris, fashion capital of the world."

The clatter of the door interrupted her. Abigail flew into the room and threw herself onto a chair. "Sorry."

Clapping and cheers erupted from the rest of the

team.

"Nice of you to join us." Shona turned back to Nina. "No one's going anywhere. Your wardrobe will have to wait. Now can you lot stop admiring the surroundings and park your backsides?"

The sound of chairs dragging across parquet flooring signalled their compliance and added to Shona's headache. She pulled a couple of paracetamol from her pocket and swigged them down with water from one of the plastic bottles in the middle of the room. Following the renovation a ban on drinks and food had been put in place. There was a book out on how long this would last. Peter was currently odds on favourite with a week. Shona placed a fiver on two days. She knew her team too well.

"So, what's the skinny on the search at the crime scene?" Shona gazed around her.

The room remained silent

It lasted a few seconds, then, "So skinny you can't see it." The team busied themselves laughing at Nina's witticism.

"Ha, flaming, ha. Would you like to repeat that to the chief? See if he finds it funny?"

"It's been bone dry round there for weeks. The fog overnight didn't put a dent in it, so not much to see," said Iain.

"Neighbours?"

"Pretty remote around there, Ma'am," said Peter. "Hence the Bothy. It provides shelter in a blizzard or inclement weather."

"She could have been sheltering from the fog and went inside," said Jason.

"In those shoes? Not on your life," said Nina. The horror on her face matched the scandalised tone in her voice. "That woman went up there for a reason, and I'd bet a month's pay on the fact that reason was a man."

"Could be a woman," said Abigail.

"Aye, we're equal ops when it comes to murder round here."

"We're the real police, not the PC police. Focus boys and girls."

"I've no' been called a boy for a long time."

"I'd say she was up there for a tryst and whoever she met offed her," said Roy.

"Instinct tells me you're right. Officialdom tells me we keep our options open." Shona rapped her laser pointer on the table.

"And those options are, Ma'am?" Abigail raised a quizzical eyebrow.

"Completely diddly squat that's what they are." She contemplated her water bottle for a minute then added, "But it's our job to search them out and consider the clues. So have at it."

"Our instructions, Ma'am?"

"Roy, on HOLMES, find any similar M.O.'s. Iain, you're on forensics. Get everything off to the right department. The rest of you, sift through anything brought back from the hillside. There has to be something other than sprigs of heather."

More high-pitched chair scraping as the team hurried off.

"Peter, wait."

Her sergeant turned round.

"You and I are interviewing Jock. He should be replete and ready for a chat by now."

6

The rancid smell of unwashed bodies hung in the air as they entered the room. The result of too many collars and a reformed tramp whose habits hadn't caught up. The ban on drinks in the briefing room didn't extend to interview rooms. Jock was ready for a refill on his tea. Shona sent Jason to fetch drinks. He returned with the brews, and a gargantuan slice of chocolate cake for Jock.

"You treat a man well, Shona. Nice brekkie, followed by a wee bitty cake. I'd marry you if your heart didn't belong to the procurator fiscal."

Shona's laughter filled the room. "Jock, I think I love you. However, I'm a one-man woman. As you say, Douglas has my heart."

"If he ever dumps you…"

"You'll be the first person I turn to, Jock."

Peter coughed. "Time's marching on, you pair."

Shona raised an eyebrow. "Who made you the boss of me? You're right though." A sweep of the hand, "Peter, our witness is all yours."

Peter leaned over and placed his forearms on the table.

"How often are you up near that particular bothie, Jock?"

"Quite a bit. It's a bonnie walk and I can always get a cuppie when I arrive. A bowl of water for Fagin, as well. Stayed a night or two at times."

"Have you ever seen anything suspicious?"

"No' really. Sometimes a wee shi…" He looked Shona in the eye. "Pardon my French. Some wee toerag will be up there getting up to nae good."

"What sort of no good?"

"Drugs, Sometimes battering his lassie around. Showing her who's boss."

"Did you report this?"

"Nah. Gave him a black eye to match the one he'd given his girl."

Shona butted in. "You might not want to say that in here, Jock. It's called Assault to Injury around these parts."

"Aye, I'd gladly take my punishment."

"The toerag's not reported it so we'll leave it there."

Peter took over again. "Do you think he might have gone so far as to kill?"

"Your dead wee lassie is way out of teorag's league."

"Seen anything else in your rambles with Fagin?"

"A few nights ago," He screwed up his face, "Fagin went nuts. Started barking at shadows."

"Did you see or hear anything?"

"Nope. Stupid mutt was probably barking at a badger or a hedgehog."

"Do you know what night?"

More face screwing. "Friday, maybe Saturday night. Sorry, I've no clue what's going on."

Shona took over. "That will be all, Jock. Could you keep your ear to the ground? Stay away from bothies in the meantime." She stood up. "Peter, make sure Jock gets a lift back to his flat. Pop into my office first."

She pulled fifty quid from her purse and gave it to Peter. "Make sure whoever takes him home buys groceries and toiletries. I suspect all his benefits are going on feeding the canine dustbin."

"You really do love Jock, don't you?"

"I really do."

"Big softie."

Shona smiled. "If word gets out you're toast."

Peter winked and hurried off to do her bidding.

Heads down and silence indicated the team were hard at work. They ignored Shona as she strode over to Roy's desk. It did her heart proud to know they were pulling out all the stops.

"What you got, Roy?"

"No similar killings anywhere in the U.K. A couple in the U.S.A. Separate states. Alaska and Mississippi so thousands of miles from each other."

"Not likely ours then, unless it's a copycat."

"Could be, but I'd say no. Not on the appearance of one corpse."

Shona tugged a chair over from an empty desk, and sat down. "I'd agree. Mind you, with my track record that could change any minute. So we're left with nothing?"

"Not quite. Three missing women roughly the same age and build as our lass."

"Print them."

"I'm ahead of you." He reached over to his printer, then handed Shona three sheets of paper.

Shona scrutinised the profiles. "My money lies on Debbie Smith, but the other two do bear a distinct resemblance."

"My thoughts, exactly."

"I'm off to pay Debbie's N.O.K. a visit. Fancy coming with?"

"You bet."

7

Roy drove while Shona phoned Mary.

"That's you at it again, Shona."

"I'm hoping it's a one off this time."

"I'm hoping for a fortnight in the Bahamas but it aint gonna happen. You'll be filling my drawers up with bodies before the cock crows three times."

"What's the state of play with my latest victim?"

"She only arrived a couple of hours ago. Give me a chance, I've other work as well."

"I'm only ringing to ask if she's presentable for an identification?"

"She is. I'll hold off the examination until you've been."

"You are a legend."

"Don't you forget it, Little Miss Inspector."

Laughing, Shona hung up and shoved the phone in her voluminous fuchsia pink handbag. Made by Givenchy, it was a present from her Sergeant on her return from three weeks in India. The only piece of designer apparel that Shona owned, the cost made her uneasy.

Debbie's parents lived up a closie in Provost Road. In Dundee, closie didn't mean a close up selfie for social media, but a traditional tenement. The entrance greeted them with peeling paint held together by graffiti. The Smith's lived at the top, four stories up. As they trudged up the worn stairs, they held their noses against the eye watering smell of ammonia. Drunks and closies were never a good pairing. Shona thought fondly of her own brightly painted front door, and well kept apartment complex.

The Smith's door had a fresh coat of paint. The smell of urine gave way to one of bleach as Shona and Roy stepped across the wet concrete floor of the landing. In the absence of a bell, Roy rattled the letterbox.

A woman answered the door. White hair and dark bags under her eyes, with swollen ankles forced into slippers which had seen the blades of a pair of scissors.

"Aye?"

"Mrs Smith?"

"That's me. I'm not religious and I'm not interested."

Shona showed her ID and Roy followed suit. "Detective Inspector Shona McKenzie. May we come in?"

"What's up? It's Debbie. She's dead isn't she? I knew—"

"Mrs Smith, we don't know." The thump of heavy footsteps reverberated up the stairwell. Shona wasn't keen to hold this conversation in public. "Can we discuss it inside please?"

The door opened further. They traipsed inside and sat on a well-worn chintz sofa.

"When did you last see Debbie?"

"Six months ago."

"Six months! You didn't report her missing until four weeks ago." Shona sat up straighter.

"I spoke to her five weeks ago. She always phoned on Sundays. When she didn't ring I called you lot."

"What did your daughter do that stopped her visiting you? Did she work away?"

The woman lowered her head and mumbled. "She was a pole dancer down at yon nightclub in town."

"Cat's Eyes?"

"Aye, that's the place."

Shona filed this away in a mental filing cabinet. One that was labelled, Alexeyevs.

"I'm sorry to say we have found a body." As tears filled the woman's eyes, Shona added, "We don't know if it's Debbie's. We need you to come and identify the body."

The woman aged a few years, right in front of their eyes.

"Is there anyone who can come with you?"

"My other daughter. Lydia. She's sleeping." While they waited for Lydia to get ready Shona called to warn Mary they were on their way.

She had the body ready and Shona accompanied Mrs Smith and her daughter to view it.

Lydia grabbed her mother as she slumped down. "That's not my sister."

"Are you sure?"

"One hundred percent." She walked over to the body and moved the hair aside.

"You can't touch—"

"My sister had cancer. Her hair grew in thinner and there were still some patches of hair loss." She turned towards her trembling mother. "It's not her, mum. It's okay."

The young woman laid a gentle arm around her mother's shoulders, and led her off.

"I guess it's on to number two," said Roy.

"I guess it is. Mary we'll be back."

Cara Ballieri's N.O.K. lived in a terraced house in Charleston. Two cracked steps led up to the peeling front door. Another rap on the door and it was opened by a man, unshaven, his only clothing boxer shorts.

His glower was followed by, "Piss off." The closing door met the full weight of Roy's body.

Shona shoved her ID in unshaven's face. "DI

Shona McKenzie. We need to have a quiet word with you."

"Your goon nearly broke my door." He stared at a hand so large it resembled a bunch of bananas. "And my hand."

"My goon, as you so delicately put it, was carrying out his duties in a diligent manner. Now, are you going to let us in?"

He stomped off leaving the door swinging wide. Shona and Roy followed.

The sitting room was decorated with beer bottles and very little else.

"We're here about your daughter."

"I hope you've come to say you've found the ungrateful bitch. She owes me money. Meant to give me some every week but she never appeared."

Shona and Roy stared at each other. A slight rolling of Roy's eyes and a nod of Shona's head was all that was needed.

"I am sorry to say that we have found a body. It may be that of your daughter. Please could you come to the mortuary to identify her?"

Shona choked back the words she really wanted to say.

This time they hit pay dirt. The body Cara Ballieri's. Her father's only take on the matter, "Who'll gi' me money now?"

"You might want to try something unusual, such as working," said Shona.

"Stupid cow." His face resembling a purple party balloon, he lunged at Shona.

Roy stopped his progress. "Calm down, Sir."

"We'll forgive you that outburst given you are grieving. One more and you'll be enjoying the comfort of my cells."

He answered questions on Cara's employment and friends. Apart from the fact she was a student nurse and he'd only met one useless tosser of a boyfriend, he knew nothing about his daughter.

Once he'd gone, Roy said, "If he gave up the beer he might have a bit more money."

"Couldn't agree more."

"One question I'd like answered. How did a student nurse, from a background like hers, afford designer pearly whites and clothes?"

"Yet again, you ask the right questions, Ma'am. It's impressive."

"Stop toadying."

Shona dispatched the two female sergeants to the University and Ninewells Hospital. Their brief, elicit the maximum amount of information on Cara Ballieri. The pair hurried off, chattering and laughing all the while. Nothing would keep them down, thought Shona.

A wee visit to Cat's Eyes was needed. This time it would be in the cold light of day, rather than covert by night. Owned by a pair of slippery Russian gangsters, it seemed to feature in most of her investigations. With skin like *Liquiglide*, charges just ran off them and rushed into the gutter. Shona was always up for a tussle with the Bobbsey twins. Leaving Peter in charge she dragged Jason and Iain along with her.

"I think I can manage seein' as I'm only in charge of Roy."

"Roy's more than enough for anyone to manage. Keep him out of trouble." She glanced in Roy's direction. Head down he was banging on a keyboard like it was a personal mission. It probably was, knowing Roy.

8

A couple of seedy pensioners were Cat's Eye's only customers. They were ogling a beautiful young woman plying her wares just inches from their noses. One man's hand moved and Shona averted her eyes. She didn't want to know where it was going or what it was doing.

Shona threw a glance at her detectives. "Eyes front, boys. You're here as muscle, not to take in the surroundings."

"She's stunning. What's she doing this for?" said Jason.

"More money than we'll ever see I would think."

Iain glanced back at the dancer and her watching pensioners. "Not much of a way to earn a living though."

"Wouldn't do it for all the money in Scotland."

A pair of designer suits and expensive loafers appeared in front of them. They were occupied by a couple of blonde haired Russian Adonises.

Before Shona had a chance to open her mouth, one of them said, "You are persecuting us, again."

"I've not said anything yet. We've tipped up looking for a chat and maybe a coffee and a couple of sticky buns." Shona lounged nonchalantly on the bar.

"What's this talk of sticky buns? We sell only alcohol and not to you."

"Keep your shirt on sunshine. We're here to chat, not eat. A couple of cokes wouldn't go amiss though."

"Better make it clear it's the drink we're talking about, Ma'am."

"Good point."

"This is legitimate business."

"So you keep telling me. Why don't I believe you? You're missing a dancer?"

"I have so many."

"This one's called Debbie Smith."

"Not one of mine."

She pulled out a photo from her bag and shoved it in front of his nose.

"Never seen her."

The movement of his eyes said otherwise.

"You're lying like a rip off Russian watch. Have I got to take you pair down to the station? Again."

A couple of 'gentle' police hands stopped Gregor's lurch forward. Stephan glowered at Shona. She waited it out.

"I was mistaken. She is Raven."

"Raven! She's blonder than you pair."

"She wore a wig for performance. Created more allure."

"A sound business decision then?" The sarcasm in Shona's voice was thicker than the recent fog. "When did you last see her?"

"Four, maybe five or six weeks ago. She took her pay and left."

"This didn't bother you."

"My dancers are free to come and go as they please."

"Were you expecting her back?"

"Next night. I was one dancer short."

"Diddums. Lose money, did you?"

Stephan crossed his arms and the glower deepened. The more time he spent in Shona's company, the more the look was perfected.

"Was she with anyone in particular that night?"

"Many men."

"I said, in particular. Would you like me to get a Russian translator?"

"No." The room shook at the volume.

Shona abruptly straightened up. "Thank you, gentlemen. That will be all."

She turned and walked towards the door. "PC's Roberts and Barrow, are you coming?"

Jason trailed behind her to the car. "I'm confused."

"Me too."

"We're off to get a warrant for any video surveillance in that club – overt and covert."

"You're a clever woman, Ma'am. The Army would be proud to have you in their ranks."

"How'd you think she got to Detective Inspector, Soldier Boy?"

Sherriff Struthers divvied up the warrant with his usual warning. This was not to bring any further dead bodies to the city.

"I shall do my level best, Sir." Shona was long past the stage of arguing about her reputation in this area.

Shona's stomach told her they'd missed several meal times. She arranged for uniform to go and do a search and retrieve of Cat's Eye's. They were always up for a bit of chitchat with the Brothers Karamazov. The day had taken it out of her. Heavy eyes and slumped shoulders indicated the team were not faring much better. She released them from the shackles.

"I'm off for a pint. Anyone else?" Jason's military background meant he worked punishing hours and partied like the glitterati. Neither situation seemed to faze him.

Roy grabbed his jacket. "Count me in. I need to get wasted."

"Before you complete that action, remember we've a case. I need you bright eyed and bushy in the morning."

His face fell but he said, "Got it."

"Anyway, I thought you were past all that. I seem to remember something about a girlfriend and a toaster."

"Turns out the toaster was too boring for her. She dumped me."

"Did you say she dumped you?" The surprise in Nina's tone was unprecedented. Roy usually discarded his girlfriends.

"I'm not surprised. I've always said you were a dreary git.' Never one to miss an opportunity to throw a barb at his nemesis, Jason was quick off the mark. Relations had improved between the pair but, like the friendship between the USA and Russia, there was always a bubbling undercurrent.

Roy punched him in the arm then rushed out the door. "Last one in the Goosie Gander pays for the first round."

The room emptied. Shona returned to her office to get her jacket. She might as well join them. If nothing else, she might be able to stop Roy drinking himself into a coma.

Goosie's was packed and flea ridden. The clientele was made up of anyone and everyone from Bell Street Station. As she shuffled through crisp and fag packets to get to the bar, Shona strongly suspected no self-respecting criminal would be seen dead in here. Plus, saying you planned a heist in the Goosie Gander didn't have the right street cred for a crim. Hence the reason it was the favoured haunt of the polis as they were called around these parts. A large Talisker was placed in her hand as she arrived at the bar. Looked like she'd be calling her wee cousin to drive her and her car back to Broughty Ferry. Thank goodness for relatives with the ink not quite dry on their driving licence, and saving up for a car. She pulled out her phone to arrange a time for said relative to appear. She downed the drink and ordered another.

Shakespeare ignored her and sidled up to Erika, her cousin. Piteous mewing said the cat was starving and it was pointless asking Shona. Her mistress was heartless and refused to feed her.

Shona threw her keys on to the antique dresser in the hallway. Pulling off her jacket, she folded it over a chair in the sitting room. She bent down and tickled the cat under the chin. "You're a phony kitty."

The moggie responded by turning her back on Shona, her tail ramrod stiff. The cat, named Shakespeare, turned out to be female and refused to answer to any other name. She ruled the roost and tolerated Shona's presence in her house.

Erika vanished inside the spare room and shut the door. Shona suspected an iPad and Facetime were involved in her disappearance. *Conversation obviously needs an added cash incentive.*

"Looks like it's just you and I puss."

She went to open a tin of luxury salmon cat food.

9

Shona left a note for her cousin saying she would run to work. Erika should bring the car to Bell Street and hand the keys in to reception. The teen's parents lived in a flat in town, so she'd be happy with the loan of the wheels. Before hurrying out the door, Shona returned and added to it. The girl had the car for the day. She could return it at 6 pm.

The run was both energising and stunning. The Tay river put on its finest silvery display. A couple of dolphins cavorted in the water playing to their audience of one. This early there were only trudging cleaners and post office staff on the streets. The remainder of the city continued their slumbers. Arriving at the office she showered and grabbed her one emergency set of clothing. A posh frock and jacket, it was meant for TV interviews.

The heat was crucifying, even this early in the morning. She shrugged off the jacket and hung it on a hanger. Mug of coffee in hand she wandered through to the briefing room to review the previous day's evidence. Bang slap up to date from the previous night's input. She'd brought along the surveillance tapes which were plonked on her desk. The accompanying note said the Alexeyevs were raging. She made a vow to stay away from dark alleys for a few weeks. Other than that, she decided the Alexeyev twins' feelings were not her problem.

Switching on the fan, she turned it down low. A maelstrom of crucial evidence would not lead to an orderly case.

The female sergeants were thorough in their research and information covered the boards. Wandering over, Shona took a slug of coffee and nearly spat it out as she burned her mouth. Jason had pocketed the dosh from the sweepstake on the food and drink ban. Gulping in cold air, Shona studied Cara Ballieri's life. A good student, and outstanding nurse, she shone on the wards. Caring and compassionate, patients loved her. Out of work she kept to herself and her colleagues didn't know a lot about her. A couple of close friends, both off duty, but addresses provided and in a file. No mention of a boyfriend. Shona took another swig of coffee and jotted down some notes. What in this girl's life led to her being murdered half way up a Scottish hill? There had to be something. What about her dad? A nice lass, coming from stock like him. Did he bump her off? On second thoughts, he wouldn't slaughter the cash cow. Did he have insurance out on her? Highly unlikely, but no stone and all that. Good questions, and all rattling around in Shona's overactive brain. Shona intended finding the answers.

By the time the others pitched up she'd downed three mugs of coffee and drawn up a list of tasks longer than the Tay Road Bridge. She'd also sneaked down to the canteen for some sustenance before Peter and his healthy eating appeared. Talking of Peter.

"We seem to be missing a senior sergeant. Any clues as to his whereabouts?"

"Had something to do on the way. He'll be here in about twenty minutes."

"Nina, how come you have this vital piece of information, and I don't?"

"I have my phone on me, and you don't."

Laughter rang around the room amidst a bunch of

fist bumps.

The corner of Shona's mouth turned up in a wry smile. "When you're quite finished having fun at my expense."

Amidst shuffling and coughs, they settled down and grabbed pen and paper. Or the electronic version thereof. A chunk of money appeared from who knows where and ginormous phones were purchased. The kind that functioned as diaries, notebooks, and every other bell or whistle they could ask of it. Shona was sceptical of the security aspects but those in the know assured her they were on super duper extra strong lockdown. Also, the chief ordered them to use them. No right of appeal.

"Jason, find out where Cara's dad was the night she was murdered. Roy, check up on life insurance. Nina and Abigail, interview her friends."

They all shot off leaving, Iain. "You and I are on security video."

He groaned.

"It's a tough job but someone has to do it."

There were a lot of security tapes. After twenty-five minutes Shona had lost the will to live. Peter joined them giving Shona an excuse to break off.

"Where have you been?" This was said without rancour, Peter having earned the right to some flexibility.

"St Ninians, getting weighed. When it comes to putting on weight, I'm not sure if I'm more scared o' the doctors or the wife."

"Isn't there a Slimming World group over the water?"

"Aye, but there's no way I was going there. Fiona lets me get weighed early and shoot off."

"Now you're here there's security footage awaiting

your full attention."

"Punishment? That's enough to give a man a relapse." He plopped down next to Iain who hadn't taken his eyes off the screen.

"Good footage, Ma'am. Nice and clear."

"Anything of Debbie Smith?"

"Everything of Debbie Smith. She leaves nothing to the imagination." He grinned.

"Get your mind out of the gutter, PC Burrows. You know what I mean."

"Apart from the dancing, nothing so far."

"Keep at it. I'm off to see Roy."

She detoured via her office to check her emails. *How can anyone get a hundred and fifty freaking emails in two short hours?*

She highlighted most of them and with a satisfyingly firm click of the mouse, they disappeared into the ether. After answering the most important ones, she stood up.

The phone rang. She grabbed it, "DI McKenzie."

"It's the duty sergeant."

With those words, Shona knew she was on the move again. Not once had the man phoned with good news.

"What have you got for me?"

"Your needed down at the Howff."

"The Howff? Graveyard? The last person to be interred there was about a hundred and sixty years ago."

"I believe so, Ma'am."

"They're way past my tender ministrations. No one could be murdered there in broad daylight." The place was so old and famous it was almost a public park. Tourists would be crawling all over it.

"Your presence has still been requested. You've to take your team."

10

Six Weeks Previously

Lights pulsated to the beat of the music, a myriad of colours which fractured and scattered only to be replaced by others. The room, bursting with customers, radiated heat like a fifty-megaton nuclear bomb. Vintage Krug was dispensed alongside cheap vodka. No one with the price of entry got turned away. Anyway, cheap was a misnomer in this exclusive place.

Gregor and Stephan Alexeyev, dressed in identical Saville Row dinner jackets, surveyed all before them. This was their kingdom and they ruled with a rod of Russian iron. A nod of the head, flick of the wrist, or a hurried phone call was all they needed for a command to be carried out. An infinitesimal narrowing of the eyes the only indication of occasional displeasure. An increase in muscle tone as a fist is clenched. Otherwise, matching Chernobogs, the Slavic god of darkness.

The dancers writhed and swayed, around poles and on laps. Provocative poses, a slow lick of the lips, breasts tantalisingly close. Then with a mad whirl the dancer is gone, leaving the punter begging for more. Notes of every denomination are tucked in silk thongs. The money magically disappears and is replaced, over and over.

A hand reached out, fondled a breast. A hard slap to the face and she continued her dance. The man put his hand to his face, feels the heat. A suited and bow tied bouncer appeared, whispered in the man's ear. He stood up and followed him. With one glance behind him, he walked out of the door. The shadows of the night engulfed him.

The wait was long but the man patient. Still. Used to inactivity he blended into the background and watched. And waited. Pulling a cigarette packet from a pocket, the man flipped it open and pulled out a cigarette and a lighter. Once lit he took a long, slow drag, held it in his lungs for a moment, then exhaled. Almost poetic in its execution. He placed the gold lighter back in the packet and leaned against the wall in the dark alley. And waited.

The young woman pulled her pashmina around her as she left the club. Despite the heat of the day, the nights felt cool around these parts. She gazed around, no Taxi's. *Flaming typical.* She pulled off her high heeled shoes and, barefoot, began the long walk home. A movement, startled, she whirled round. "Who's that?"

The man approached.

"Oh, it's you. What do you want now?"

"To make sure you get home safely."

The woman fell into step beside him. He grabbed her hand. A slight tug on her part and then it settled into his. They walked in silence as a vague mist peeped at them from a distance.

11

Police of every possible variety packed the Howff. Sticky beakers of every possible variety peered through the railings.

"Peter. Nina. Move this lot along."

"We're no' doing naebody any harm. Fu—"

Shona's voice rose. "In handcuffs if necessary." She strode off leaving her sergeants on crowd control.

The POLSA was at the far side of the graveyard, ordering his team about.

"Any chance we could get the road shut, Sergeant?"

"Tough one. It's a main thoroughfare. The buses will go nuts."

"It's the buses I'm worried about. Anyone on the top deck can see right in here."

He considered for a minute. "You've got it. I'll let the council know."

It was easy to see where the action was taking place. A crowd of coppers huddled around an ancient grave. Shona scattered them with one word. "Move."

Iain, Abigail and Roy stared at it as though it would jump up and bite them. The heavy stone lid lay ajar. Female ankles, not looking their best, with a pair of scanty undies around them, peeped through the opening.

"If that's a corpse then it's no ancient relic."

A brace of burly bobbies dragged over a tent and started to unfold it.

"If you don't mind stepping away for a couple of minutes, Ma'am? We'll have the area screened in no time."

Shona left them to it and went to get kitted up. Her team followed.

"Females first then the rest of you."

She slid inside the tent, followed by Nina and Abigail. Slipping off her dress she climbed into white coveralls and emerged into dazzling sunlight.

"Hades has to be cooler than this."

"I can assure you it is. I feel like I've been to hell about a hundred times since I started this caper." Roy gave her a little salute. "No disrespect, Ma'am."

"You'll be going there again if you carry on with your cheek."

His response? Throw back the tent flap and disappear inside.

The weathered, moss covered grave was above ground. More like a crypt than a grave, the solid lid hadn't been moved since 1889. At least that was the date of its last legal occupant.

"Lift the lid off. I need to see what's in there."

"We can't, Ma'am," the POLSA said in her ear. "It's illegal. We need a warrant and a cleric of some description."

"And your boyfriend. He'll be here any minute nae doubt." A fully suited Peter joined them, appearing from nowhere like a svelte ghost. Shona was impressed as he'd previously resembled a blimp.

"Her boyfriend, as you so nicely put it, Sergeant Johnston, has arrived."

A rush of blood to the face signified Peter's contrition.

Douglas laughed. "Don't sweat it, Peter." He turned to Shona. "Your boyfriend also brings the warrant." He pulled a form from his pocket.

"There's a vicar on his way as well, Ma'am."

"What's he supposed to do?" Shona shoved the hood of the suit back and tried to blow on her own face. "He can inter us. We'll all have died of heat stroke before he arrives."

"If you're talking about the vicar, I'm a she."

Shona whirled round. "Sorry. I've never been so glad to see anyone, regardless of their sex."

They all grabbed an edge of the lid and lifted. Startled by a shriek they dropped it back down again. The lid cracked and a corner fell off.

"You can't do that."

"Who the blazes are you, and who let you in here?"

"I'm the cemetery custodian and I let myself in. Or I would have done if the gate hadn't been swinging wide this morning."

With an imperious wave of the arm, Shona summoned a policeman.

"Take Mr…?"

"Lemon."

"Mr Lemon, somewhere for a cold drink. Let me know where you are and I'll join you when I'm finished here."

"But… ludicrous… my…" His voice faded into the distance as the copper led him off.

"Let's try it again. On three. One. Two. Three."

They gently leaned the lid against another grave stone, and surveyed the body inside the tomb.

"Is Mary on her way?" Hands on hips, Shona gazed around her. She bent down and peered inside the tomb. Insects scurried every which way, startled by the sudden exposure to the glare of sunlight.

"We called her, Ma'am. Thought the police surgeon would be a bit redundant."

"No kidding. Jump to it, do a search of the area. Iain, photographs. A slow sweep. Anything you find get a flag down, photographs then bag it."

Peter took over. "Search in squares. Nina, South East, quadrant." He divvied up the other quadrants amongst them and the search started.

Shona tapped her foot and squirmed inside the suit.

After about ten minutes, Mary appeared, dressed in shorts and a sweat soaked t-shirt. She pulled it away from her body.

"Flaming road works. Thought I'd never get here. Car air con's given up the ghost. I'm in purgatory."

"You aint seen nothing yet."

Mary bent over and examined the young woman who lay before them. She didn't have to bend far given her diminutive stature. They say the dead look peaceful. This dead body looked horrified.

"Definitely dead. Time of death difficult due to the heat. Not long though."

"Do you think she was dead when she was popped in the grave?"

"Just about. Do you see the marks?" Mary pointed to the victim's mouth.

"She was suffocated. A shiny new pound coin says I'll find fibres as well."

"My shiny pound goes on this wee lassie being the missing, Debbie Smith."

As they spoke, Iain was busy clicking away with the camera.

"Point that thing in another direction. You'll crack the lens taking photos of us in these outfits."

"I've been asked to get some images for the new recruiting brochure, Ma'am."

"Take any more pictures of me and we'll be recruiting for your job."

"Speak for yourself, Shona. I was quite enjoying

my five minutes of fame."

Shona stripped off her outfit and poured herself back into her dress. She ran her hands through damp hair. Leaving the victim in Mary's more than capable hands, she went to find Peter.

"Are you okay in this heat?"

"It's gruelling."

"Get changed. Roy can carry on with your area." She shouted over a couple of graves. "Abigail, take over the crime scene."

Abigail nodded and carried on with her search.

As they exited through the gate, Shona banged into an elegant black woman, wearing a bright orange dress. All five foot ten of Shona looked up into the laughing face of Adanna Okifor, a reporter for *The Dundee Courier*.

"How did I know you would be sniffing around?"

"Come on now, Shona. You know we're pals."

Shona smiled. "Pals is a bit strong. Let's say I'm more likely to tolerate you these days."

"I'll take what I can get. What's the skinny?"

"Police Scotland are dealing with an incident in the Howff Graveyard. More details will be released at a press conference."

"This I could have done without your input."

"Go figure." Shona followed Peter up past the timeworn stone walls of the cemetery.

12

They retired to the air-conditioned coolness of a local café. Most of the city being on holiday, it was blessedly quiet. Grabbing a couple of cold drinks, they sat down beside their witness. Shona was glad to see that Peter's face had resumed a more normal hue.

She stretched out a hand. "We'll need you to come to Bell Street. Give us a statement."

"I won't be doing much else, given your cluttering up the place I should be working."

Shona slugged down the rest of her diet coke and stood up. The two men followed suit.

Bell street resembled a pressure cooker. Someone had obviously been to Argos. Numerous brand new, high powered fans had appeared. Shona took one into the interview room, along with Peter and the custodian.

She leaned over and switched on the recording device. "Interview with Mr Simon Lemon, DI Shona McKenzie and Sergeant Peter Johnston in attendance."

"Mr Lemon, please talk us through what you found?"

"I went to the Howff at 9 a.m. as always. Opened the chain on the gate."

"You said opened the chain. You mean the gates were closed?"

"Locked up tighter than the Honours of Scotland."

"Sorry?"

"The Scottish Crown Jewels. You're not from round here?"

"I am and I'm not."

His look said she was half baked.

Shona's look said handcuffs.

Peter jumped in. "There's a way in through a couple of the shops. Back door leads on to the graveyard."

"Thanks." She turned back to the witness. "Does anyone else have a key?"

"There are three keys in existence. I have one. The council have the other two."

"Who would have access to them."

"I'm not sure. You'll have to speak to the council."

"I intend to. What did you do next?"

"I cleaned up some crisp packets and fag ends. Then—"

"What did you do with them?"

"Threw them in the bin." The 'You're an idiot' look was back.

"Peter, ring Iain and tell him to bring the bin bags back with him."

Peter left, pulling out his mobile phone.

They waited until he returned. Simon Lemon lounged in his chair, one leg crossed over the other.

For someone who found a body not quite three hours ago he's pretty relaxed.

"I walked around the place checking to see if there were any repairs needed. Some of the graves are beginning to fall over. I noticed that one before I got to it." He swallowed a couple of times.

Not as cool and collected as he gives out.

"Would you like some water."

"No, I'm okay. The minute I saw the grave had been disturbed I called the police."

"Did you touch anything?"

"No. I left, locked the place up and called you from the street."

"Well done. Thank you. Please leave your details in case we have any more questions."

"Peter, get on to the council and find out about those keys."

"Will do. I'll also take a gander at the shops. The council offices are one side of the Howff, the shops the other. Won't take too long."

"Dundee, the biggest village in the world."

Shona headed in the direction of the shower. *How do the police do this day in day out in hot countries? I hope they're paid well.*

Shona took the chief a cold drink and a pastry in the hope it would placate him.

"Inspector, I have had quite enough of this. Can you not go one day without attracting a serial killer?"

"In all fairness, Sir—"

"I don't want to hear it. Get this case solved, and do it quickly."

"Sir—"

"Dundee has the highest crime rate in the country."

"Sir—"

"The UK. Do you hear me, UK?"

"But—"

"They are currently investigating us, so get this solved. Now."

"May—"

"That will be all."

"Yes, Sir."

She was talking to the chief's bald head again. End of conversation. She ground her teeth so hard she was astonished the boss couldn't hear them. Anger, blue flame strong, filled her head, shoving out all thoughts of hericide.

The anger, and thoughts of a stiff Talisker, carried her through the next twenty minutes. By then she'd calmed down enough to speak to the others. Twenty minutes in which she could have been investigating the case. Instead she'd returned to plotting the chief's demise. She was a hair's breadth away from researching crypts in the farthest flung reaches of Scotland. There must be a remote island somewhere that could be pressed into service. This cheery thought brightened up her day and gave her renewed energy to carry on with her task.

13

While she waited for the others to return, Shona
returned to the CCTV footage. Iain had taken copious
notes which she studied. Several men appeared on
multiple occasions during 'Raven's' performance.
Debbie Smith obviously had a fan base.

Shona resumed where Iain left off. Peering at a
screen being back breaking work, she sat back and
stretched. A thought struck her. She picked up her
mobile and dialled a number.

"Dundee City Council, how may I direct your
call?"

Shona asked about CCTV cameras around the
nightclub. There were two in the nearby vicinity. Shona
requested the tapes of the night of Debbie's
disappearance. It appeared the Council had gone all
digital. The digital files would be emailed to her within
the hour. *Awesome. Score for Dundee City Council.*

The rest of the team returned from their labours, hot,
sweaty and ready to drink the sea dry. Shona insisted
that they down several glasses of water. Dehydration
and heat do not make a good mixture.

"Grab yourself some lunch. Then back here
soonest."
The stampede out of the door could not have happened
faster.
Peter raised a quizzical eyebrow. "You think we'll see
them any time soon?"

"They better be back soon. Get down there in about
ten minutes and round them up."

Peter said he would go down there, grab them both

a sandwich, and drag the others back to this sweatshop.

Lunch knocked back, and water bottles in hand, they headed to the briefing room.

"What've we got so far?"

"Very little, Ma'am. It's been bone dry here for weeks. The ground's as solid as the tombstones. A herd of elephants could trample around in there and we wouldn't know." Iain's face had a beaten look.

"Add to that the place is practically a public park. Half the world go there and eat lunch." In contrast, Nina had a grin the size of India on her face.

"In a graveyard? Dundonians never cease to amaze me."

"Folks have a wee seat on the graves while they eat their picnic."

"What?"

"The Chinese have been doing it for centuries, Ma'am. We commune with our ancestors."

"Could this conversation get any weirder? What *have* we got? Apart from picnickers."

"We've got the rubbish bags from the cemetery winging their way to a lab," said Iain.

"Let's wait for the results from there."

Photographs of the grave and the young woman's body had joined Cara's photos.

"They're like two peas," said Roy. "Beauties."

"There is a pretty close resemblance," said Shona. "Do you think it could be another serial killer?" Her eyes took a faraway look.

The silence could have been cut with a knife.

Shona's gaze and attention returned to the room.

"Not again ma'am," said Jason. His tone said, 'oh no'. His face said, 'bring it on'.

"I'm not inclined to think so," said Shona. "The M.O. seems completely different." She paused.

An expectant hush filled the room. Shona's face told them there was more.

"Besides, I've clocked something interesting on the club CCTV."

Chatter broke out.

"Hush." She clicked a remote. A writhing mass of humanity filled the screen as they were transported to a typical night in Cat's Eye's."

"Crystal clear." The awe in Roy's voice took over the room. "They must spend a fortune on their kit."

"There are a few too many cameras in that place. It's more like invasion of privacy than security." Shona pushed another button on the remote and the picture zoomed in.

A bald man sat staring at a dark-haired dancer. They watched for a few minutes as he continued staring. Not a muscle of his body moved. Then, the dancer swayed in his direction and a hand snaked out and grabbed her breast. Without breaking stride the dancer smacked him hard on the face, then moved away again.

"That's our missing Debbie Smith, A.K.A. Raven."

"The man turned, hand to his face. They got a clear picture of him before he was grabbed by collection of muscles loosely disguised as a bouncer.

"Looks like we've got ourselves a possible suspect, Ma'am," said Peter.

"You don't happen to know him, do you?"

"Nah. Looks a bit o' a sad sack."

"Let's find him and see if he's a sack capable of murder. Peter, take the boys and hit Cat's Eye's. Get a name from them."

"It's seven pm, Ma'am."

"What? Go home from there. I'll see you all in the morning."

14

Shona stepped from the shower and dried herself with a deep pink, Egyptian cotton bath sheet. Wrapping it round her she walked towards the bedroom.

Hair dried and up in a stylish chignon, Shona applied mascara. Her long lashes thickened, the deep blue of the makeup bringing out the colour in her eyes. They sparkled at thoughts of the evening ahead. Rory and Alice cruising with their grandparents, meant she and Douglas could spend time alone. A real grown up date. Her chest tightened, her breathing quickened. She stepped inside a sapphire blue sheath dress and pulled it up. As she dragged the zip up the material settled, hugging her tall figure. At the ring of the doorbell she slid her feet inside a pair of Christian Louboutan shoes. Borrowed from Nina Chakrabarti they were far too high. Finding her centre of gravity, she moved to the door and pulled it open.

"Douglas."

Always smartly dressed, he appeared positively sartorial, this evening. His eyes widened.

"Shona, you look ..." He couldn't find the words. Actions took over as he swept her into his arms. Given her current balancing difficulties, it was more her falling than his sweeping. No more words were necessary as his lips touched hers.

Douglas's breath caught. "I've booked a table at Cosmo's"

Exclusive, and expensive, it was impossible to get a table at Dundee's newest restaurant.

"Give me a minute." She kicked off the shoes and ran into the bedroom. She returned wearing footwear she could walk in.

Douglas's smile lit the room. "Let's go." He took her hand and tugged her through the door. With a thunk it closed behind them and their date proper started.

Shona cut into her steak and blood oozed out.

"I'm surprised you can eat that with your job."

She speared the juicy morsel on her fork. "I don't notice the difference to be honest." She popped the steak in her mouth and chewed. Swallowed. "Not that there's much blood in this case so far."

"Maybe, we could avoid talk of death, tonight." He put down his knife and fork, and pulled a package from his pocket.

Shona's smile lit the room. The cares of the day slipped away.

15

Nina catapulted through the door of Shona's office, rescuing her from an avalanche of paperwork.

"Is there a reason you never knock? Seriously, woman, slow down."

"Sorry."

If a face could look any less sorry, Shona had never seen it.

"Wow. That necklace is stunning. Where did that appear from?" Nina leaned over and lifted the dew drop diamond from Shona's neck. "That's the real McCoy."

"Douglas gave me it last night."

"He's a nice chap, your Douglas."

"Did you come here for a reason other than to quiz me about my love life and jewels?"

"I bet you wished it was an engagement ring."

"No I flaming didn't. If I ever get engaged I don't want it to be associated with a murder investigation. Was there anything you wanted?"

"We're all here and ready to crack on."

Shona stood up. "Then crack we shall."

"Did you get a name from the Kalashnikov twins?"

"Funnily enough we did. Coughed it up the minute we asked," said Peter.

"What? I thought you'd have to beat it out of them."

"They were like new born lambs. I think they're a bit fed up with our boy, Humphrey Masterton. Gave us his address as well," said Roy.

"What a god-awful name. Sounds like humping masturbate."

"Jason, that is quite enough."

"Yeh, stop lowering the tone, Soldier Boy."

"Roy, you can shut up as well. The pair of you go and fetch Mr Masterton. If he doesn't come meekly, charge him with sexual assault."

"I don't think you can do that, Ma'am, not if he was in a lap dancing club," said Abigail.

"Do you think he's up on the finer points of the law?" Shona's tone indicated no response to the question was needed.

Roy and Jason leapt up.

Abigail bit her lip. The boss ploughed her own furrow and sometimes it was a little wavy.

Shona and Abigail returned to the Smith's flat. They collected Debbie's mother and sister and took them to the morgue to identify their relative. The wails gave them their answer. The corpse and Debbie Smith were one and the same person.

"I can assure you. Mrs Smith, I will do everything in my power to find your daughter's killer. You have my word on that."

The assertion sounded hollow, even to Shona.

They delivered the grieving Smiths back to their flat. Shona sat them down and explained the nature of Debbie's discovery. Given Adanna's presence at the crime scene it wouldn't be long before it was reported all over the local rag anyway. That was no way for them to find out. Her voice gentle she talked them through what had happened to Debbie, and what the next steps would be. She wasn't sure how much Mrs Smith took in. She looked like she'd closed in on herself.

"When will we get the body back? Mum and I need to arrange the funeral."

"That could take some days I'm afraid."

Silent tears filled the woman's eyes and ran down her face.

"I truly am sorry for your loss, Lydia, Mrs Smith." She handed over a card. "This is my direct number. Ring me if you need anything."

"I hate this part of the job, Ma'am. The look of despair in the relative's eyes makes me sick to my stomach."

"It's not got me turning cartwheels either. We'll need to get them in later to ask more questions. Let them grieve first."

"Jason, is Mr Masterton in an interview room?"

"No, Ma'am."

"Soldier Boy, you'd better not be yanking my chain."

Jason opened his mouth but Roy jumped in to defend him.

"He refused to come."

"And the reason you didn't bring him in handcuffs?"

"Mr Humphrey Masterton," Roy stood to attention, "O.B.E, was at work. He's a bank manager in that new one in town."

"What? The humongous one the Americans slipped in while we weren't looking?"

"Spirit of co-operation, Ma'am." Jason took over again.

"I know. It's actually a good thing. Shed loads of jobs and all that. Is our boy American?"

"No, he's English."

"That can't be the reason he's not getting impatient in one of our interview rooms."

"He said he wasn't there and, therefore, can't leave the bank. He has an 'important' meeting." Roy used his fingers to emphasise the word important.

"We'll see about that. Boys, you're on again. Follow me."

They did just that while she grabbed her jacket from the office. Then, marching back to the briefing room she snatched a photo off the wall. "Let's go."

"I don't fancy Humphrey's chances," said Nina.

Shona was too far away to hear it.

16

Shona stormed into the bank like a rhino in heat, Roy and Jason trailing behind her. Customers scattered as she strode through the impressive main hall. A converted shipping office, the bank had kept all the original features, giving it the grandeur of yesteryear combined with modern functionality.

"Can I help you?" A bank employee, somewhat puzzlingly wearing a kilt, stopped them.

Shona whipped out her ID card and shoved it in his face. "I would like to see Mr Masterton please?"

"Mr Masterton is busy. Can I help you?"

"That's very kind but, no. Take me to Mr Masterton."

"I'm afraid—"

"Unless you want to be arrested for hindering the police in the course of an investigation, you might want to take me to your boss."

The kilted man whipped a card out of his pocket and headed off. "Follow me. I'm not paid enough to take the rap for anyone."

"This isn't the Bronx. We're not going to arrest you for nothing."

Shona opened the door and strode through. Fifteen pairs of eyes snapped round and stared at her.

"How dare you interrupt my meeting?" A bald man in a Saville Row suit slammed his hand on the mahogany table.

"Keep your hair on."

By this point the man looked like an aubergine. He took a step towards her.

"Mr Humphrey Masterton?"

"Yes. What does it have to do with you? I'm calling the guards." He snatched his mobile phone from the table and pressed some buttons.

Shona walked slowly towards him and slammed her ID card on the table, followed by the photo. She could take him on when it came to fist crashing.

"Is this you?"

He spoke into the phone. "No. It's fine. My mistake." He looked around the assembled group, staring at the tableau. A fair few smirks were in evidence. "You may go."

A small woman, with ginger hair, and sporting a black polo neck spoke up. "Humphrey, you may think this is your meeting, but remember who's boss."

He turned to his colleagues. "Please stay. We will continue once this is sorted out."

With a shuffling of chairs the gathering settled down to watch the show. One of them leaned across to her neighbour. "Best meeting I've been to, bar none."

Shona looked Humphrey Masterton in the eye and said in a loud voice. "I am arresting you under Section 14 of the Sexual Offences Act 1956, Indecent Assault on a Woman."

The meeting went wild. Jason whipped out some handcuffs and attached them to the man's wrists, and he was led away.

Shona followed behind listening to the triumphant chatter. *Not a popular employee then. That'll rattle his bank vault and jolly glad I am too. Maybe I could pop him and the Chief in a bank vault and forget the combination.*

"I want a lawyer."

"Of course. PC Barrows, take Mr Masterton to ring his lawyer, then chuck him in a cell till he gets here."

"That's outrageous."

"Oh, Shut up. I've had to listen to you whining all the way here. I've had about as much as I can stomach."

"You'll pay for this. I'm going to sue you for every penny you've got."

"Sue away. You'll get about £1.49 as that's as much as I've got. The police don't make out like bandits."

"Why does his lawyer have to be Angus Runcie? Surely there has to be more than him and his sister practicing law in Dundee?"

"Aye, Ma'am." Peter winked at her. "But Runcie and McLuskey love persecuting you."

"I'm sure you're right. I'd love to throw the pair of them in a cell. Keep them out of my face for a few weeks."

"I'd help you do it, Ma'am. Only the wife gets stroppy if I'm no' home for my tea. They wouldn't let me out of nick, even for Mrs Johnson."

"Horlicks. Let's go face Runcie and his client. I'm in the mood for a wee fight."

"Stay cool, Ma'am. High blood pressure's no' good for you."

"You arrested my client in the middle of a highly important business meeting. Humiliated him."

"If your client hadn't caused such a stramash and lied to the police, we would just be having a chat with him." She glared at Humphrey. "In his own time."

"My client wants to cooperate fully."

"I'm sure he does. He's still being charged with assault."

"Assault. Are you addled? How did you come up with this rubbish?" One corner of Humphrey's mouth moved up in a supercilious smirk.

Shona pushed three photos over the table. Slowly.

Masterton looked at them. "It's a lap dancing club. Their tits are millimetres from your nose."

Shona curled her hands into fists. Ordered them to stay down, well away from the slimy git's face. "That does not give you carte blanch to touch them, squeeze them or in any other way manhandle them."

'Everyone does it. Ask the dancer."

"That would be difficult. She's dead."

Humphrey's chair slid back and Peter stood up, ready to grab him.

"Dead! What do you mean dead?"

"You might be a whizz at numbers but your obviously as thick as a mealy pudding when it comes to words."

Humphrey gave a low growl. His lawyer put his hand on his clients arm. Humphrey shrugged it off.

Shona continued. "Dead. Deceased. Is no more."

"What's that got to do with me?" The smile turned to horror as realisation smacked him like a four-ton truck. "No. No way. You can't frame me for this."

"What are you suggesting? You arrest my client for assault. Now it's murder. Do you lot even know what you are doing?"

"Oh, we know exactly what we're doing. You on the other hand…"

"How dare—"

Shona's gaze focussed on their suspect. "Where were you at 0200 on the night of 17th September?"

"How the fu—"

"Now, now, Mr Masterton. Keep it civil. No need to lose your temper."

Humphrey slowly exhaled. "How am I meant to remember that?"

"You jolly well better give it a good go, or you'll be facing charges of murder."

"I told you—"

"And I'm telling *you*. Think about it."

He pulled out his phone. Opened an app. Studied it.

"Today, would be good." Shona tapped a slow beat on the table in front of her.

"I went straight home after I left the club. There's only so much humiliation one can deal with."

After you were thrown out on your ear you mean.

Peter caught her eye. His look said he was thinking the same thing.

"Can anyone vouch for this?"

Humphrey twisted his wedding ring.

"My wife. I'd rather you didn't speak to her."

"You should have thought of that before you, and your over excited libido, visited a strip club."

"It's not—"

"Whatever. I'll be contacting your wife."

His voice turned whiney. "My wife has mental health issues. It may tip her over the edge."

"I'll take a psychiatrist with me." She turned to Peter. "Put lover boy into a cell until I get back."

"My client is cooperating fully. He doesn't need to be in a cell."

"He's still under arrest for sexual assault." She paused and stared at the lawyer. Her eyes moved to his client. "And a possible murder charge." Switching off the recording equipment she stood up. Peter moved toward their prisoner.

"You can't do that. I didn't murder—"

"Would you shut up? You're giving me a headache. If your wife gives you an alibi, you're off the hook."

Humphrey's wife looked like a half-shut knife. According to her husband she suffered from manic depression. This was as far from manic as it was possible to get without being tucked up in a hospital ward. The minute they mentioned her husband's name, silent tears rolled down her face. Shudders shook her body, yet not a sound uttered.

"Are you all right?" Shona put a hand out to the woman, who shrunk back.

"Where's Humphrey? I need Humphrey."

What on earth do I say now? No alibi, equals no Humphrey. Shona motioned to Peter to join her in another room.

"She's way over the edge. News of lover boy's arrest could push her down a chasm so deep she'll never recover."

"I'll find out who her GP is and give him a ring."

Peter hurried to the car. Shona sat with the woman, with not a word exchanged. About an hour later, Peter reappeared with a young man dressed in shorts and a pink polo shirt. He was accompanied by an older woman sporting crimplene, and mopping her face with a lace edged hankie.

The man showed an NHS Scotland ID. "Duty community psychiatric team."

"Could you examine Mrs Masterton? Ascertain if she's fit to be questioned?" She and Peter left them to it.

"It's a bonnie area this." Peter gazed around him.

"It certainly is." Well-kept lawns and rose bushes

preened to within an inch of their lives, were the predominant landscape feature.

"It's no' often you see an Army Nurse Fuschia round these parts. Wonder if she was one herself?"

Shona was saved from answering this enlightening statement by the appearance of crimplene.

"What did you want to ask her?"

"We need an alibi for her husband. Is she up to it?"

"Let me put it this way. If your case rests on her indoors, you're stuffed."

"I guess her husband will be enjoying our hospitality for a bit longer then."

"Yep, and in about two hours she'll be enjoying the private wing of Surehaven hospital in Glasgow."

"Thanks for your help. I truly hope Mrs Masterton recovers quickly."

"Nosy neighbour time."

"Aye, Ma'am."

Ten minutes later they had their answer. A combination of nosy neighbour and concerned friend had him off the hook. For murder, anyway.

"That gentleman lowers the tone. Tumbled out of a taxi, cursing fit to wake the devil. I went out and gave me a piece of my mind. He told me to go to Forfar."

"What time?"

"Midnight. His poor wife. I stayed up and kept an eye out. She may have needed refuge."

"Has she needed it before?" Peter drew himself up to his full height. .

"Several times. That horrible man has her driven mad."

"In what way?"

"She comes over here sobbing fit to break your heart. Says he's not come home and she's worried something has happened to him." She looked like she'd stepped in dog muck. "Drink and loose women are the only thing that's ever happened to him."

"Have you seen him with other women?"

"No, but he smelled like the inside of a whore's en suite the other night. It doesn't take one of you lot to add up the sums."

"You've been very helpful. Thank you."

As they walked back to the car, Shona asked, "What's in Forfar?"

"Nothing. Why?"

"Humphrey told nosy neighbour to go to Forfar."

Peter's bellows could awaken the dead. "Shona, you never cease to amaze me. It's a polite way of saying go to fu—"

"Okay. Okay. I get the picture." A rosy hue crept up Shona's face.

Then a giggle started and in the space of a heartbeat her laughter joined Peter's. As they walked back to the car several curtains twitched. Obviously not a neighbourhood for noisy laughter.

18

They returned to the Gulags via the bakers and purchased several large cream cakes. This solidarity with Peter could only take her so far. In a nod to his healthy living he bought a small fruit slice.

"I'm not sure that's particularly good for you."

"It's better than the mountain of fat and pastry you're about to scarf down. It's the only unhealthy thing which will pass my lips this day."

Her scathing look did not go unnoticed.

"I'm a changed man, Shona."

Mary had left several messages for Shona to ring her. She grabbed a bottle of water and headed for her office, a fan and the phone.

"What's up, Mary?"

"You're a hard woman to pin down, Shona McKenzie."

"If I could stay in my office and still solve cases I'd be in investigator's heaven."

"You've more problems than you think. Your lassie in the crypt, Debbie Smith. It looks like she was raped post mortem."

Shona's stomach churned. Her mouth couldn't seem to form any words.

"Shona." There was a pause. "Shona."

"Sorry... I'm sorry." She grabbed her bottle of water and slugged some down. "That's disgusting."

"It most certainly is. You might want to prepare yourself for the next bit." She cleared her throat. "I'd say it happened in the cemetery."

Shona gagged. Sipped some water. "Thanks. I

wouldn't want your job for all the whisky in Scotland."

"Sometimes I wish I worked in a supermarket. I get through by telling myself I'm doing good."

"If she was raped there must be semen. At least that's good news."

"If you're pinning your hopes on that, you're stuffed. Used a condom. Common type you can buy in any machine in a toilet."

"Why can't I ever get a break?"

Shona pressed end and slammed the phone down. *If it's the last thing I do, this sick pervert is going to be behind bars for a very long time. If there's any justice in this world the other inmates will torture him until his dying day.*

She took a deep breath and stood up.

The intervening hours hadn't improved Humphrey's mood. His lawyer's mood was even more foul if that were possible.

"Why have you held my client here for no reason?"

"You're beginning to get on my nerves. Where did you get your law degree? I gave you plenty of reasons why your client is in my custody."

Shona turned her back to the lawyer and gazed at the prisoner. "It seems you're off the hook for murder."

"My wife gave you an alibi?" His eyes blazed hope.

"I'm afraid not." Her voice became gentle. "I'm sorry but we had to call out the duty psychiatrist to your wife."

He leapt to his feet.

"Please sit down. She's being well looked after." Her tone remained low as she explained his wife's current whereabouts.

He thumped back into his chair and put his head in his hands. Sobs escaped through his fingers.

"It's apparent you love your wife."

"More than you know." His sobbing intensified. "That's why I go there. To the club. My wife and sex don't go together."

Shona sat back in her chair and gazed at the man. She took a deep breath. "You're free to go."

Humphrey looked up. "What!" The squeak in his voice could crack glass.

"You're right. It's pretty much a sex club. I'll put the fondling down to a lapse in judgement."

Humphrey stood up. "Thank you so much."

"Keep your hands to yourself in future."

As he left the lawyer trailed behind him. Runcie turned to Shona. "I will be reporting you."

"Again? Crumbs you're keeping my boss busy."

"You are outrageous."

"Yep. I sure am. Toddle off now. Your client's waiting."

Runcie slammed the door of the interview room behind him.

The smile on Peter's face reached his hairline. "You're for the high jump when the Chief finds out."

"I know, but baiting Angus Runcie is worth the bollocking."

19

It took just twenty minutes for Shona to be called to the chief's office. She wasn't feeling quite so cheery by the time the tongue-lashing was over. Sacked and demoted were the two words she remembered most clearly. She resolved to keep her tongue still for a few days until the boss had cooled down.

"Sod the lot of them."

"Anyone in particular, Ma'am?" Abigail came around the corner just as Shona uttered the words.

"Anyone with a higher pay grade than us. What have you lot found while I've been pissing off lawyers?"

They carted coffee and cakes to the briefing rooms, disregarding all rules about drinks and food.

"Try not to get it on the carpet. They'll bill us for it."

Roy gazed at his feet. "Bit late, Ma'am. Cream's not good for shag pile."

"Leave it be. We'll get Mo on the case. Focus."

Thumps and cup banging heralded their settling down.

"Nina, what was the deal with Cara's friends?"

"Quiet lass on the whole, but the life and soul of the party if she got a drink in her."

"Did they spill the beans about what she might be doing the night she disappeared?"

"They're not keen on dishing the dirt. Tried every which way and not a peep."

"Get them in and I'll have a go. An interview room might rattle them enough that something pops out."

"Now."

"Yep. Go get them. Jason, go with her."

The pair swilled down the dregs of their coffee and departed.

"Righty ho, Roy. What have you got on Cara's loving father?"

"Spends all his money on booze and fags. He was in The Rabbie the night Cara disappeared."

"Verified?"

"Barman remembers him. He was drunker than a sailor when they splice the mainbrace. Carried home and chucked on the sofa by one of his pals."

"To be honest I didn't think he'd choke off his main source of income. No stone and all that though."

When she updated the team on the sexual activity on Debbie Smith you could have heard a feather fall.

"After 30 years there's no' much'll shock me. That's one o' the few things."

Emotion deepened Peter's accent. Shona didn't have the heart to pull him up for it. She'd got the gist of the point anyway.

Thigh deep in paperwork, Shona sighed. Management had its moments but it was mainly boredom squared. She was saved from committing career suicide by the return of Nina.

"Courtney, the very epitome of a spitting tabby cat, is currently occupying our interview room."

"Ask her if she wants a coffee. It might cool her temper down."

"A rag stuffed in her mouth might do a better job."

"Nina. Say that again and you will be on a report."

The minute Shona stepped in the room she wished she had that rag.

"How dare you? This is police intimidation. I don't

have to tell you anything. I want a lawyer. You'll be trying to fit me for her murder. I'm not having—"

The crash of Shona's fist on the table stopped her mid flow. "Shut up. Give us a chance to speak."

"This—"

"What part of shut up didn't you understand? We're not trying to frame you for anything. We're trying to get to the bottom of what happened to your friend."

"I don't know what happened to her. That's your job."

Despite the bravado, Courtney's hands shook.

"We just need to ask you a few questions. Are you happy to do that?"

"Whatever." She blinked away tears.

"Thank you. Do you know where Cara went the night she was killed?"

"No." Her eyes darkened.

"I think you do."

"I don't." The corner of one eye twitched. She put up her hand to stop it.

"Who was she with?"

"I don't know." Her foot started to drum a tattoo. She held her knee down with her hands.

"I've had as much as I can stomach. Tell us now or I'm arresting you for obstructing a police officer."

Tears overflowed and rolled down Courtney's cheeks. "I'll get chucked off my course."

"For heavens sake just tell us. No one is going to get chucked off their course."

"She was going out with Barry Grisham."

"Who's he?"

"He's in charge of our training."

"What? How old is he?"

"He's sixty three." "She looked up and added hurriedly, "But Cara loved him."

"I'm sure she did." Shona kept her tone mild.
"Thanks, Courtney. You're free to go."

"Can I have a lift back?" She looked at Shona's
face and added, "Please?"

"Sure. Nina, come with me and we'll drop
Courtney off at the nurses' home."

"Once they were in the corridor, Nina said quietly,
"Is a voice recorder needed?"

"It most certainly is."

Shona returned to her desk and slipped a pair of
handcuffs in her pocket. It always paid to be prepared.

20

Fifteen seconds of Barry, and Shona was ready to throw him in a cell and drop the key in the river Tay. All smarmy smiles and oily voice, he made Shona itch.

"Beautiful ladies, I will do anything to help you. Anything at all. You just have to ask."

"You can start by calling me Inspector, and my colleague Sergeant."

"Of course." The smile grew even smarmier.

Nina had a look in her eye that said she was about to kick him in the unmentionables with her pointed Prada. She took a step forward but stopped when Shona laid a hand on her arm.

"Mr Grisham. May I ask, is that your real name?"

"Of course, everyone asks. It is my dea…" He took in Shona's look and said, "Inspector. John is a very dear cousin of mine."

Shona felt heartily sorry for John. Although she suspected he was no relative of Mr Smarmy. Not even distant.

Shona looked round the room. Full to brimming with staff at computers the noise was unbearable. "Is there somewhere quiet we can go?"

"Follow me."

The small tutorial room barely held two people, never mind three. Shona shifted her knees slightly so they weren't in proximity with Barry's. *I can se he'd have no trouble getting up close and personal with his students.*

"Cara Ballieri. Tell us about her."

Grisham rocked back in his chair at Shona's abrupt

tone.

"There's no need for that. We can stay civil."

At one look from Shona, Nina bent down to readjust her shoe. Shona leaned so far forward she could smell the man's rancid breath and see his nicotine stained teeth. "Listen here. Keep that acerbic tongue of yours under control or you'll be spending life in Barlinnie. Answer my questions and nothing else. Capiche?"

She sat back in her chair. "Mr Grisham, we would like to record this session. Are you happy with that?"

"No. No way. I'm trying to help you."

Shona pulled the handcuffs from her pocket. "Would you like to do this down at the station? I'm sure your colleagues would love to see you being escorted off the premises."

"Fine."

Shona switched on the recording and gave the usual preamble. She added, "For the record, Mr Grisham has given his permission for this session to be recorded."

"I was threatened with handcuffs."

Shona shook her head. "Barry. Barry. You should have taken up creative writing instead of nursing." Her voice changed. "Now tell us about Cara Ballieri."

"What do you want to know? Anything to help find her killers."

"When you last saw her for a start?"

He frowned and after a few seconds said, "About three weeks ago. I visited her on the ward."

Shona changed tack again. "What was she like?"

"A lovely girl. Quiet. Reserved. Kept herself to herself."

"When did you pair start dating?"

"What are you implying? How dare you?"

"Implying? I'm stating a fact."

"We were not, as you say, going out."

"I'll interview every single person in here and every student nurse. That should get to the bottom of it."

Barry's eyes narrowed. If looks could kill, Shona's mother would be speaking to an undertaker right now. "Okay. We were. I was trying to protect her reputation."

"For heavens sake, she's currently lying in a drawer in the mortuary. Her reputation is the least of her worries." She took a couple of deep breaths. "When did you last see her?"

He pulled out his phone and gave it a couple of brisk taps.

"Last week."

"Which day?"

"Thursday."

"I think you'd better come with us to the station." She took in his pale face. "Don't worry there will be no handcuffs involved. Unless you try to make a run for it that is."

"I'll come." Not quite so smarmy now. Evil blazed from his eyes.

Shona shivered despite the heat.

21

Five Weeks Previously

The streets were quiet. No one around except one young lad leaning against the graffiti covered wall of a run down shop. Dressed in baggy jeans and a t-shirt, it clung to his ripped body. He raised one hand and lazily swept a long blonde fringe out of his eyes. The other hand stayed in his pocket, surreptitiously holding the jeans up.

The size of the jeans was a necessity. A tool of his trade; a trade usually associated with women. Yet, it was as old as time for both men and women. He offered his wares to male or female, whoever had the necessary hundred quid. His stomach rumbled. Business had slowed recently. It was too hot for sex and summer meant only a few meagre hours of darkness. He moved, settled against the wall once more.

Maybe he should change his pitch. This place wasn't the best for trade but he was desperate. He looked at his watch. A Gucci, he'd nicked it from a customer. This particular theft wasn't going to be reported to the police, but he'd thought it best to keep out of the way for a few weeks. Hence his standing in this godforsaken spot.

"It's been long enough. My mark's long gone back to his hole."

A rat scurried off at the sound. The only audience to his words, it didn't want to pick a fight.

His brain told him to make a move and his feet

followed. Despite his better judgement the need to feed himself was greater. This being summer, it would be light by 3.30 am.

His feet and his brain took him to the centre of town. Modern concrete edifices jostled with ancient sandstone buildings. The juxtaposition of old and new portrayed Dundee's past and present in a packed tumble of streets and alleyways. There would be rich pickings when the clubs emptied. He found an ideal spot, near the one working street lamp, and settled down to wait. A few people scurried past. Clubbers, they weren't interested. A few old women ghost like in the flickering light of a broken street lamp. He thought about them going to their jobs as cleaners. More casualties of life's misfortunes.

An old tramp trudged up the road, turned and held out a dirty beer bottle. "Wan' some?"

The teen shuddered. "Nah. You're all right, Pal. Thanks though." His mother always said he should be polite. That was before she kicked the bucket and left him with a mountain of debt and a six year old to look after. *God, I hope Charlie's okay,* He'd left him tucked up in bed; sucking his thumb and cuddling stuffed rabbit. At nine he was a bit old for all of that, but it was the only comfort he got. The rest of his life sucked big time.

Another twenty minutes passed and he thought about going to the skips behind the supermarket. See if he could get a box of cereal. Anything to get food for the wee man. He took a couple of steps, then stopped.

A man approached, tall, imposing and regal. His muscles matched that of the young man awaiting his arrival. Sure steps carried him up the street. Slowly. This was a person at home in his own skin. Sure of himself. Dressed to perfection in an outfit that was definitely not off the peg. Unless the peg belonged to a New York fashion house.

The young man pulled himself to his full height. Showed off every rippling muscle to perfection. The hair drooped over one eye, giving him a mysterious look. He gauged the man before him and made a split second decision. He bowed his head slightly and gave his prospect a coy look through his fringe. His appearance now changed his age downwards.

"How much for the whole night?"

A quick look at the attire and a rapid calculation. "Four hundred quid."

"I will give you five hundred if you stay for breakfast."

This would keep him and Charlie in food for months. The decision was a no brainer. Charlie would be fine. He'd manage to eat the last bit of dry cereal and take himself to the library not five hundred yards from his house. They'd give him a glass of milk and a biscuit. They always did. "It would be my pleasure," he said. The punters liked a bit of posh.

The deal sealed they walked up the street towards the waiting car.

22

Barry was escorted to an interview room and provided with a plastic bottle of cold water. Witnesses dying of heat exhaustion weren't a good look. Enquiries about air conditioning were currently in operation. The Chief's take on it? It would be cheaper than 24/7 fans and the cost of bottled water.

Shona popped into the squad room. "Did we ever get an answer from the council re CCTV outside Cat's Eyes?"

Several pairs of human eyes stared at her. The room looked like a demolition company had taken up residence.

"I've no' had anything. What about you lot?" Peter's gaze swept the room, and took in a lot of head shaking.

"I thought they were emailing you, Ma'am," said Abigail.

"They were, but I've had nothing. Abigail, chase it up."

"I'm on it."

"The rest of you get this place cleaned up. There's pigsties in a better condition."

Peter stood up. "You heard her. Grab the Marigolds." He sat down again and picked up a copy of *The Courier*. When it came to cleaning his was definitely a management role. If nothing else, it made Shona smile.

"Roy, I've a different task for you."

"How come—"

Shona didn't even look at the owner of the voice. "Shut it, Soldier Boy. I'm not in the mood for posturing or complaints."

She pulled Roy aside. "Get on the interweb and winkle out all you can about Barry Grisham. He's currently something to do with nursing. If there's even a speck of dirt I want to know about it."

"Any other instructions?"

"Go wherever you want. The dark web is all yours."

Rehydration by water hadn't improved Barry's mood. Shona wondered if he'd like a gin and tonic. She'd kill for a whisky right about now. A day of interviewing witnesses, in heat you could fry bacon in, had *her* mood in a nosedive. *Wonder if I'd get away with dumping lover boy in a cell for the night and shoving off home?*

Given that the chief expected her to solve the case, an early knock off wasn't an option. That would leave her with knocking Barry's block off. Metaphorically speaking of course. The smarmy git was in for it if he put one foot wrong.

"Mr Grisham, thank you for coming in. We would like to ask you a few questions."

"I want a lawyer."

"Why do you want a lawyer? You're a witness."

"I'm not talking without a lawyer."

"Good grief. You've had the entire journey here to make the call. Why now?"

"I didn't want you lot listening in."

"Done something you don't want us to hear?" She sighed. "Take this idiot to phone his lawyer."

Twenty minutes later Angus Runcie confronted her again. "My client is innocent."

"In a town of a hundred and fifty thousand people how come there are only two lawyers? Stupid ones at that. We've not accused your client of anything to be innocent of."

"Why is he here?"

"Witness, although his behaviour's making me want to change my mind. Fast."

"You said you saw Cara last Thursday? What did you do?" continued Shona.

"Had a curry at the Bengali on the Perth Road. Then went for a drink at that new wine bar."

Pretty honest and upfront so far. Maybe a bit too upfront. "What time?"

"How do I know? I wasn't timing things."

"Did you do anything after that?"

"No. She got the bus home."

"Very chivalrous of you."

"Feminism and all that. Modern women, eh?"

"Stinking men who leave little girls to make their own way home. You can bet your bottom dollar I'll be checking all that out."

The back and forth continued with no useful information presenting itself. Shona was about ready to bang Barry's head off the table. Or at least her own head.

"Can anyone vouch for your whereabouts after Cara supposedly got the bus?"

His eyes shifted left indicating he was lying through his teeth. "No. I went home."

"If I find out your stretching the truth you'll be done for murder."

"You can't threaten my client."

"If you think that's a threat you ain't seen anything."

The minute she got home she poured a large Talisker whisky. This case, and the heat were going to turn her into a drunk. Shakespeare wound round her legs purring fit to bust. Shona wondered what the cat had been up to which put her in such a good mood. The purring turned to pitiful mews of the 'I'm starving' kind. She opened a tin of salmon cat food. The pampered moggy took one sniff and demanded something else.

"You'll eat it. I've better things to spend money on than feeding you."

The cat sat beside the bowl and stared at her. Shona gave in and opened a can of lamb. This was more acceptable to the cat's palette. Shona refilled her whisky glass, making sure it was a generous measure. If she got called out, a taxi or a lift was on the cards.

She wandered through to the living room and plonked herself down on the comfortable overstuffed sofa. She pulled up her legs and picked up the Sunday Times telly magazine. The cat jumped up on the sofa, licked her lips, turned round three times, curled up and fell asleep. The shrill ring of the phone shattered the peaceful scene.

This had better be anyone other than the duty sergeant.

23

It was not to be. "Ma'am, You've a shout out. They want you at the Eastern cemetery."

"Another cemetery? What's going on in this city?"

"We never had such goings on until you arrived, Ma'am. If you don't mind me saying."

"I jolly well do mind you saying."

She put down the phone and decided to run to the Eastern. Sweating the whisky out of her system seemed like a good idea. She'd hitch a lift back from one of the others.

Arriving hot and sticky she banged into Nina at the gate. She was sporting the supermodel look, with heels to match.

"I was about to go on a date."

"I'm sure Erik the Viking, will wait for you. I'm sure our latest corpse isn't worrying about your love life."

"His name was Leif, and well you know it."

"Your use of the word was leads me to conclude you are no longer dating."

"Why can't you keep up?"

"Probably because your love life is more convoluted than Spaghetti Junction."

"I'm going out with a Spanish dancer. He's got a body like a Greek God and a huge—"

"Nina, that's enough. TMI."

"Pair of castanets. I was going to say pair of castanets."

"Is that a euphemism?"

"No it flaming well isn't. I shan't tell you any more

if you're only going to take the piss."

The cemetery held more people than Piccadilly Circus at rush hour. All these bodies in a cramped space didn't do much for the crime scene, or Shona's state of mind. Fast approaching dusk, intensified the menacing shadows that were the coppers.

"Get this lot out, and some lights in."

"Eddie's on his way, Ma'am." The POLSA, used to Shona's posturing, gave her a lot of leeway. Most POLSA's would have kicked her to Forfar.

"Why is it always Eddie? Does the man not sleep?"

"I've got him on speed dial in case you need lights. He insisted."

"Hooray for Eddie. The man's a saint."

The team stood by the back wall well away from the crime scene.

"Here, Ma'am" Peter handed over a couple of plump cherries.

"I can't believe you brought a snack to a shout out. That beggars belief even for you."

"I didn't bring them. I picked them."

"What? Where from?"

"The tree you're leaning on."

Shona looked up. Several ripe cherries hung from the low branches.

"Seriously. Only Dundee could have a cherry tree in a cemetery."

"Best wee city in the world, Ma'am. Full of surprises."

"More surprises than a body ever needed."

"Not that bodies are anything we need to worry about finding."

"Hah, flaming hah." Her phone rang and she pulled it out of her pocket. "McKenzie."

"Douglas. I didn't recognise the number." She

listened. "The dog ate your phone? You need to get your mongrel under control." Listened again. "Yep. I'm on a shout. Are you coming over?"

"Your poor mum. I absolutely understand she can't look after the kids. Shingles on a cruise isn't good." Listened again. Her voice husky she said, "You too. See you soon."

"I take it your boyfriend's mum's not feeling so chirpy, so he's not coming out."

"Got it in one. Not that it's any of your business Nina Chakrabarti."

"Of course it's my business. I'm your friend. It's enshrined in law that I need to ferret out every single piece of information about your love life."

"You are so dead."

Eddie appeared and they were soon working by the light of thousand watt bulbs. The Eastern being in the midst of a built up area, they probably had half the neighbourhood up and looking in.

Shona was expecting to see another crypt. This was more of a raised up grave. According to the moss-covered gravestone, the last occupant had been interred 91 years ago. So why did this grave look newly dug and covered over? The most likely story, the grave was legit and another internment had taken place. However, this would not involve the police and a fully-fledged crime scene.

"What's unusual about this grave that merits my getting out of my pyjamas?"

The POLSA was quick with an answer. "Gravedigger, Ma'am. Called it in. It was rocketed up the chain given there's already one body been found in another man's grave."

"Where is he?"

"*She* is at the lodge."

The gravedigger looked about twelve, but given her profession must be at least eighteen. She took in Shona's look and said, "I'm twenty-seven, and yes it was my chosen career path. I've been helping my dad dig graves since I could hold a shovel." Her weary tone indicative of the numerous times she had been asked these questions.

"Good for you. I like a woman who knows what she wants." Shona showed her ID card. "DI Shona McKenzie. You gave us a yell. Why?"

"There's a funeral tomorrow. The woman is a hundred and sixteen. Oldest resident of Dundee until she shuffled off to meet her maker."

"Do you usually dig graves at night."

"No. My 7 year old's trip to A&E meant I'm behind schedule. I popped down to get it done once he was in bed."

"And?"

"And the grave had been interfered with. My colleague's on holiday so, I'm it for any cemetery in Dundee."

"Have you got records of internment?"

She pulled forward a ledger and pointed to an entry. "Last body laid to rest in that grave was 1925. My burial's 10 year old son."

"Where's her husband buried?"

"The Somme if the funeral home are to be believed."

"Any clue as to when the latest dump might have happened?"

"A few days maybe. The turf's not had time to settle properly."

"What about the rest of this area?"

"Most of them were around about that time. An outbreak of Spanish influenza saw mortality rates shoot up. Most of the graves were filled. The odd internment since then but it's a quiet area."

"Does it get much footfall?"

"Not really. There aren't many folks left who remember these poor souls."

"Who would know this was such a quiet area?"

"Apart from the grave diggers you mean? There are a couple of semi famous graves. Two soldiers from the Crimea were buried here. War heroes by all accounts. You get the odd PhD student from the university looking for their graves. They'd know."

"You'll need to give a statement to my PC." She called over Roy and the pair wandered off to find somewhere to get it done.

24

From a window in a dark room a man watched what was happening in the cemetery. *How had those fools found the body so quickly?* The spot was carefully chosen, carefully researched, a dark corner, overhung by trees. No more bodies to bury there and the graves long forgotten. No one left to tend them, or place freshly cut flowers. Only those who cut the grass went anywhere near this place, and that had happened a couple of weeks previously. The research had been thorough.

He did not move and, unblinking, watched every move the police made. A spade was picked up and the first cut made in his newly dug grave. The spade dug deep yet again and the turf placed carefully aside. This was a reverent procedure. Even from his distant vantage point he could tell this. They, not unlike him, revered the dead. Treated them well.

The police scurried around as he watched. Ants with no plan in mind, yet, somehow the non-plan unfolded with precision and professionalism. It was easy to tell this as the scene unfolded over a period of hours. This was the perfect viewing point with no disturbances. He pulled a pistol out and fondled it lovingly. Imagined what could be done with this weapon, the handling of which had been learnt from childhood. A childhood of beatings, of scars, of not knowing from where the next crust would come. A beggar who overcame his difficult beginnings. This was no more. He held all the power.

In the corner of the large, tastefully decorated room a woman struggled against her bonds. Tied to an antique French chair she could not move far. She tried to scream but no sound made it through the gag. Maybe a whimper, but nothing more. He turned and stared at her.

"Quiet. This will go wrong if any noise is made."

The woman shrank back. Terror widening her eyes. He resumed watching.

25

Someone had contacted the Sherriff and the POLSA had a warrant to exhume the grave. A couple of gravediggers were on their way from Perth, blue flashing lights all the way. The lass from Dundee, being a witness, couldn't wield her shovel in the customary fashion. Shona was standing by the grave, fully suited, when something barrelled into her and sent her flying. Right on top of the grave, which was now a crime scene. One now contaminated by her.

"What the...?"

She attempted to struggle up, but was prevented from doing so by a heavy body and a wet tongue.

"Fagin? What the flaming heck are you doing here?"

Fagin answered by jumping up and down on her chest and resuming the licking.

"Get this bally animal away from here."

The heavy animal lurched away from her chest, barking like a dog possessed.

"Who let him in here?"

"Sorry, Shona. We were passing the gate and he hurtled off. I'm no' as young as I was and couldnae catch him."

"Jock, we can't have him running around destroying evidence." This was the sharpest tone she'd used on the auld tramp.

"I'll take him away."

She called a copper. "Take this pair down the nick and feed them. Then return them to Jock's flat." She turned to Jock. "You're lucky I'm not arresting Fagin for obstruction." One corner of her mouth flickered as she tried to maintain the grim tone.

He smiled and followed the copper. "Thanks George. You're a topper." Jock knew everyone in Dundee and they all knew him.

It didn't take much digging before a naked body was exposed, a mere foot below the surface. The gravediggers stopped and put their spades down.

"We can't go any further with this."

The POLSA walked over and said, "The pathologist is on her way. We thought we might need her."

They all huddled under the cherry tree again. Shona tholed her impatience for once, respect for the dead being more important than hurrying things up. Add to that the fact they couldn't carry on without Mary. Their white suits glowed in the fluorescent bulbs giving the impression of ghosts congregating in a cemetery. Any drunk passing by would get more of a shock than he ever envisaged.

They didn't have long to wait; giving the impression blue lights had featured in Mary's appearance as well. The good citizens of Dundee must wonder what was happening on the streets for so many sirens to be screaming into the night.

"Evening, Ghengis. Let's have at it." Mary's professionalism belied her jocular words. She was thorough and quick. The naked body of a young man lay before them, green skin and bulging eyes and tongue demonstrating his state of putrefaction. Blonde hair was starting to fall out. The cause of his death was evident by the large slash adorning his throat.

"Poor wee lad. I'll need to get him to the mortuary, but I'd say he's been here no more than a few days.'"

"Thanks, Mary. I'll leave you to it and we'll see what we can find. I'm sure any evidence will be long gone, but Ive got to make the effort."

"Good luck with that. It's a cemetery, anyone can wander in and around."

Shona sighed. "Don't remind me."

She hadn't even started with the search when she quite literally banged into Adanna Okifor.

"Has someone in the police got you on speed dial."

Adanna's gentle laugh tinkled through the still night air.. "Half the city has me on speed dial."

"I can well believe it. Go away. How many times do I need to tell you that you're not wanted? How did you get in here anyway?"

"Charm and beauty."

"Is your boyfriend on guard duty?"

"That would be telling. What's going on?"

"Nothing you need worry your pretty little head about."

"Come on. Give a woman a break."

"Look. I know I've got to a stage of tolerating you, but giving you info is more than my job's worth. Just say you were here and an extra body's been found in a grave. You could have worked that out yourself."

"Thanks, doll."

"Don't doll me. Don't mention me either."

"I never saw you." The stunning African beauty wandered off to talk to someone else."

She's like a wasp, always buzzing around and ready to sting you at any given moment.

Two hours later they were suffering from terminal exhaustion and had collected all the evidence they could. This didn't amount to much. Some cigarette ends, cigarette ash, a piece of indeterminate cloth caught on a rose bush and a silver earring. Whether any of this related to the case remained to be seen.

"Shona, I've just about had it. I can't put one foot in front of the other any more."

"I'm not surprised in those shoes. You need to stop wearing Jimmy Choo's to a crime scene."

Shona sent them all home and told then to return at 10 a.m. She hitched a lift and fell on her bed fully clothed. The morning could look after itself.

26

The morning brought a whining cat and strong coffee.

"Shakespeare, there's plenty to eat in your bowl. Stop being such a fusspot. That's all your getting."

She banged on the Tassimo machine and staggered into the bathroom. The sight in the mirror was enough to frighten the dead from their graves. Puffy eyes and a pale face greeted her. She rubbed her eyes, brushed her teeth and stepped in the shower. Liberal application of shower gel, shampoo and conditioner gave her new life.

Back in the kitchen and ignoring the cat she gulped down scalding coffee and headed for work. She took the route via the banks of the Tay, to remind herself what a privilege it was to be living in such a beautiful City. It wasn't all bad, and the sun dancing off the water made her feel glad to be alive.

She was the first one in, apart from the chief who wanted a word with her. She took him in a cup of Earl Grey tea in a china cup. Just the way he liked it. There were a couple of shortbread biscuits as the supporting act.

Her efforts were in vain as the chief was already out to get her. He threw a copy of *The Courier* at her.

Oh dear. Her urge to swear was strong but she forced herself to behave.

He didn't say one word as she read the article. This was an ominous sign as his default mode was to shout at her. The silence meant that at some point of his choosing he would start on her with the force of a power driver on the most powerful setting.

Grave Matters in Police Scotland

> Yet again Dundee is under siege from a
> serial killer. And yet again the police
> seem powerless to deal with this or
> apprehend the killer. However, although
> I do not usually defend them, in this case
> the killer is more than just one step
> ahead of them.
>
> Why are bodies being dumped inside old
> graves? This should be the question the
> police are asking, and *The Courier* is
> sure that they are asking this question.
> This does not change the fact that the
> people of Dundee are once more afraid
> to sleep in their beds at night.
>
> In a shocking twist, it is not only women
> who are being murdered, but also men.
> Gender means nothing to this monster
> bringing terror to our city. If murder
> were not bad enough, the desecration of
> graves…

The drivel carried on for four pages. It was obviously a
slow news week in Tayside. During that time the chief
sat glaring at Shona. She read through, folded the paper,
and placed it on his desk. The silence continued. Shona
waited it out.

"What have you got to say for yourself?"

"Sorry, Sir?"

"It would appear that the local press knew about
last night's find before I did."

*How in the name of all that's holy did I forget to
inform him? Digging myself out of this is going to*

require several gravediggers.

"I am extremely sorry, Sir. I didn't deliberately leave you out of the loop, but it was late, and I didn't want to disturb you, or your wife. I appreciate why you are upset, and I take full responsibility."

The chief sat back in his chair, a stunned look on his face. Then he leaned forward and put his chin on his clasped hands.

"I appreciate your candour, Inspector. Do not let this happen again."

"Of course not, Sir. I will appraise you at every opportunity."

"Now, the Chief Constable is making a visit. He is in conference with the Commissioner of the Metropolitan Police. Then he will be here by about 4 pm. I would like an update before then."

"Of course, Sir." She started to rise from her chair.

"Not so fast."

She sat down again.

"Call an official press briefing. We need to give them the real story. That will be all."

27

The desk sergeant was looking out for her, and grabbed her the minute she left the chief's office.

"I've not had a cup of coffee yet. Can't this wait? Unless you've news of more graves full of extra bodies."

"Ma'am, there's a clown waiting for you."

"For a minute, I could swear you said a clown."

"That's right. A big cuddly yellow and red one." The corner of his mouth twitched before he reined in the smile. "With large feet." The smile escaped.

"Are you having a giraffe?"

"I'm deadly serious, Ma'am." He handed over a business card. "His name, he informs me, is Colin."

"For heaven's sake. Everyone else gets normal cases. Mine are littered with clowns, sheep, puppies and yetis."

"Your cases do seem to be a wee bitty odd." He leaned over the desk. "You've livened the place up right enough."

"I'm glad I'm good for something. Is there a reason for Colin the Clown being in the station?"

"He has information for you. At least he seems to think so."

She rolled her eyes. "I doubt it. Probably some deranged idiot who hasn't got enough to entertain him." She stared at the sergeant, who held her gaze. She broke first. "Get him into an interview room."

"I'll get one o' the lads to do it. I'm no' wandering through the station with a clown."

"Your street cred's the least of my worries."

The only person who'd made it in so far was Abigail, who looked as fresh as she always did. Late nights did not seem to faze her.

"I need you to come with me. We've a clown to interview."

"Did you say—?"

"Don't ask. If this is anything to go by it's going to be one helluva day."

Shona felt like she was in a Miles Baker painting. The clown took up a lot of space. He was also psychedelic. So much red and yellow in such a confined space was a tad overwhelming.

"Colin…?"

"Mainwaring. I'm just called Colin the Clown though."

"Colin. Thank you for coming in. You say you have information for us?"

"Possibly. I was at a hen party the other night. Went on a bit late."

"How late would that be?"

"Three a.m."

"I've never heard of a clown stripper before. It's usually our lot they're emulating."

Colin pulled himself up to his full height. He could still barely peer over the top of the interview table."

"Inspector, I am not a stripper. I was merely performing my usual humorous act."

"Sorry. You have to admit it's a bit of an odd gig for a clown."

"At five hundred big ones a night, I ain't turning it down."

"Jeez, I'm in the wrong job. So, what happened at three in the morning?"

Colin's hands suddenly became of great interest to him. He studied them carefully.

"Today would be good."

He coughed a couple of times, then, "I walked past the Eastern cemetery and heard a gate clang." He shuddered. "Gave me quite a fright."

"Did you see anything?"

"I thought it was the wind, then I saw someone carrying something."

Shona almost shouted. "Did you see their face?"

Colin threw her a look that signified her stupidity. "It's a cemetery. Not exactly floodlit at night. I think it was their back."

"What did you do then?"

"Ran as fast as my size twenty fours," he waved his shoe in the air, "Would carry me, and flagged down a passing taxi."

"Why didn't you call us straight away?"

The 'you're addled' look was back. "If you did a gig at a hen party would you be sober? I thought the evil drink had me hallucinating."

"Far from it. I think you saw our killer."

He shrunk back. "What are you lot going to do to protect me?"

"Public figure like you. It's going to be hard." She took in the terror in his eyes and her voice softened. "Don't worry, we'll look out for you."

"Can you give us any description at all? What about height?"

"Taller than me."

Shona threw him a puzzled look.

"I don't mean to be rude, but everyone's taller than you."

"No need to get personal." He thought for a minute. "About six foot maybe."

"Build?"

Not fat, but not thin either. I got the impression he was strong."

"Because?"

"He was carrying a heavy load and not stooping. I have to carry a lot for my act. I'm strong but it's still a struggle."

"You keep saying he, are you sure it was a man?"

He thought for a minute, then, "I suppose it could have been a woman. The height made me think it was a man. Plus the bundle he was carrying was large. I didn't think a lass could carry that much weight."

Proves even clowns have preconceived ideas. Might be right though. She thought back to previous cases and decided to keep an open mind. Her preconceived ideas could make or break a case.

"You've been really helpful, Colin. We'll need you to write and sign a statement. Give us contact details as well."

Shona was showing the clown out the front door of the station when Adanna appeared.

"What do *you* want? I'm in serious stook because of you."

Adanna was taking pictures of the clown and totally ignoring her.

"Adanna, I mean it. Give me that camera."

"Don't worry, I won't say he's anything to do with your case."

"If one word gets out about this I am locking you up until you rot."

"Scouts honour. I'm only here to see my cousin."

"The one that gives you all your info? You know he's going to stay a PC for his whole career, and it's down to you?"

"He'll cope. He's as thick as a bucketful of mealie anyway. God only knows how he got in to the police in the first place."

Shona just shook her head.

The Chief was not amused. "McKenzie, why can't you do anything normal? You're making our force a laughing stock."

"Sir, there's not a lot I can do about the clothing choice of our witnesses."

"Don't be impertinent. Remember who you are talking to."

"Sorry, Sir."

"If the press get hold of this you will be transferred."

"I'm afraid it's a bit late for that, Sir. Where would you like me to move to?"

"Get out of my office and solve this blasted case. I've had just about as much as I can take."

"Of course, Sir."

She wondered about asking the clown to fire the Chief from the cannon in his circus act. The thought of Thomas rocketing into orbit brought a smile to her face. Sometimes she loved her job.

28

The rest of the team made an appearance. She brought them up to date with Colin and his midnight adventures.

"Why do we miss all the fun?" Jason poured himself coffee from the pot.

"Because you were late for work so, better not go there."

"But having a clown in the station. That's boss."

Roy's swaying caught Abigail's attention.

"Ma'am, I think we've got a problem."

Before Shona had time to respond, Roy thudded face down on the floor.

"Ouch, I bet that hurt." Iain hurried over to the prostrate constable.

"What's up wi' him? It's not that hot."

"I'd hazard a guess at coulrophobia."

"You what?" A puzzled frown adorned Abigail's face.

"Fear of clowns. The wee wuss doesn't like clowns."

"Jason, that's quite enough."

Roy stirred and the green tinge to his skin faded.

Shona helped him up and Nina handed him a glass of water.

"Everyone, use the name Colin from now on when talking about our latest witness."

"Thanks, Ma'am." Roy's voice remained weak.

"What was the take on the CCTV outside Cat's Eyes?"

"You're not going to like the answer," said Nina. It would appear all the cameras around there were turned off."

"You'd better be kidding."

"Nope. All turned off from inside the council system."

"Are you telling me someone in the council is our killer?"

"I wouldn't go as far as that, but could be an accomplice."

"Anyone know how many people work for the council?"

"Hundreds if not thousands." Even Peter looked downcast. "Do you want us to interview them all?" His eyes pleaded for the answer to be no.

"I'll think about the best strategy."

She turned to Roy, who was looking much more like his usual chipper self. "What did you find on our man Barry?"

"Not quite nailed it all yet. Can I have another couple of hours?"

"Sure. Tops though. No wasting time on Facetwit."

"Yep."

"The rest of us are canvassing the area around the Eastern Cemetery. Might be some insomniacs."

There was a rush to grab bottled water to take out with them. The area didn't teem with shops.

It was hot and thirsty work with little to show for it. Every last person swore they were tucked up in bed. The team returned with tempers frazzled and short fuses lit, ready to explode.

"That stupid git nearly got us killed."

Roy looked up at Iain's sharp tone, a huge swerve away from his usual meek and mild behaviour.

"If you weren't wittering in my ear it wouldn't have happened. Pity the Army didn't train you to keep your mouth shut."

"One more word out of your mouth and you'll be speaking from Ninewells."

"Both of you shut up. This instance." Shona's voice was loud enough to shake the windows.

"But—"

"He—"

"I said, shut it. Jason, utter any more threats in here and you will be transferred back to uniform."

"Yes, Ma'am."

"And you can cut the attitude. Last I looked you weren't in the crèche."

She turned to Iain, who at least had the grace to look sheepish. "And I expected better of you."

Her gaze took in the rest of the room. "Briefing room, now. You as well, Roy."

The clatter that ensued indicated their haste to do her bidding. The boss in a bad mood was never a good thing.

29

Roy took the floor, whilst everyone else recovered his or her temper.

"Our man, Barry Grisham isn't all he seems. His name's not Grisham for a start."

"You don't say? Dish the dirt then." Nina had recovered her equilibrium and was back to her usual ebullient self. She chucked a bottle top at Roy. "Don't keep us in suspense."

This had the desired effect of making the others laugh and chatter broke out.

"Silence in the court." Even Shona had to smile. This bedlam was better than bickering and anger. "Barry's surname?"

"Jones, from Cardiff. Got into bother with the demon drink as a brand new nurse. Nearly got himself struck off."

"Jeez. My sister's a nurse. They drink more than we do," said Jason. "She's usually the last one left standing when we're all comatose."

"I bet she doesn't turn up to work staggering, slurring and then cops a feel of the patients. Especially the ones in a coma."

The gasps were almost palpable.

"That's gross," said Iain.

"Obscene." Abigail had a look of wanting to throw up in the nearest plant pot.

"How, in the name of goodness, did he get away with that?" asked Shona. Surely that would be instant dismissal?"

"You'd think so. Goodness was what saved him." Roy looked down at his notes. "Claimed his poor old mother was dying from cancer, which it turned out she was. Said he was the only breadwinner for eight siblings, all younger than him."

"Bit of a convenient sob story. Doesn't excuse sexual harassment on vulnerable adults."

"He was made to go to AA, and it would appear he actually turned over a new leaf."

"So why the name change?"

"Did a disappearing act from mum and the weans the minute all the fuss died down."

"What a ba… bar steward." Iain summed it up for them all.

"Changed his name by deed poll and moved to Scotland."

"Wales's gain is Scotland's loss. We can't exactly arrest him for being a complete prick." Shona's tone said she'd like to bury him at sea. "Find something else on him. I can't believe he's reformed that much." She stopped and her eyes narrowed. "Let's see if we can find out what Barry the Bar Steward was doing after Cara apparently went to catch the bus."

The roars of laughter brought the Chief in.

"What is going on in here?"

They froze as his eyes swept the room.

"Inspector, may I have a word?" His low tone was menacing despite his polite words.

"Of course, Sir."

He held the door for her. As he was about to follow her he turned back to the room. "I expressly remember sending a memo banning all food and drink in here." He stared at them just past the point where they started to shuffle. Then swivelled and walked out of the room.

"I think Shona might just be in the deepest shitake she's ever encountered."

For once Peter didn't have the energy to give Roy a bollocking for over familiarity. His choice of words would have been stronger.

"It is now 2 pm and I have heard nothing regards the press briefing."

Oh my Lord. I knew there was something.

"Sir, I've been following leads and it slipped my mind."

"Unless your next words are the leads led to an arrest, then I'm not interested."

"Afraid not."

"It's too late for today. Make it 9 a.m. tomorrow and the Chief Constable will be giving it."

"Absolutely, Sir. Good idea."

"You will be in attendance. Now is there anything more I need to know?"

"No, Sir."

She was talking to the air. This left her thinking about feeding him to the bears at Camperdown Wildlife Centre.

She returned to a briefing room that had undergone a thorough spit and polish. Just when a double strength espresso would have slipped down nicely, she was reduced to water again.

She slammed into her chair so hard it rattled across the parquet flooring and she caromed into the wall.

"Grief! What a day. Did anyone find anything on the house search? Please tell me you did?" She rolled the chair back and sat down gingerly.

Most of the team shook their heads. Nina said, "One woman said she heard something like chains rattling. She said, and I quote, 'reminded me of Marley's ghost.'"

"Oh, bring a few spectral beings in why don't we. Circus performers and now ghosts."

"The chief'll love that one."

"I'm sending you in to tell him Roy. Traffic will suit you."

"Did our ghost loving witness have anything else to say for herself?"

"Thought she saw the cemetery gates swinging in the wind."

"And she didn't report this?"

"She's a crime writer. Thought her subconscious was offering up a plot. She wrote it down and went back to bed."

"And probably slept the sleep of the dead, untroubled by spectres."

"Just about sums it up. Didn't see anyone and heard nothing more."

"Abigail. Jason. Take yourselves off to the council; see if they are missing a bunch of cemetery keys. Also, check out who had access to the CCTV camera's."

"Peter, peruse missing persons and see if there's anyone that looks like our dead body."

"OOh. Peruse. Posh aren't' we?"

Shona shook her head.

.

30

Carrying a steaming mug of coffee, Shona headed in the direction of Iain's lair.

"How are things coming along with forensics?"

"I'll start with the bothy." He clicked a few keys and a file opened up on his laptop.

"Probably best. Clue's in the cemeteries will be like chasing dust motes."

"We've got a number of fingerprints. I ran them through the database and three names came up."

"Any reason why we've not got them in an interview room?" The sarcasm in Shona's voice could double as industrial paint. The heat had her temper as frayed as the rest of the population of Dundee.

"One of them is already at Her Majesty's pleasure in Perth. Went in there three days before Cara was killed." He clicked another key.

"Not him then."

"The second one is a woman. Pearl Harbour."

"Are you for real?"

"I think she's Susan on her birth certificate. She's only ever been called Pearl."

"You seem to know a lot about her."

"Same school. Dundee's tiny. However, she got a hiding about a week ago and is still in HDU. I phoned Ninewells and no access for interviews yet."

"Number three?"

"Can't find him. He seems to have disappeared."

"Name?"

"Scott McLuskey."

"Anything to do with Margaret?"

"No clue. Roy would be your best bet for that one."

"Flaming great. Keep on it."

Shona decided to ask Peter about the relationship between Scott and Margaret. He'd come up with the answer a damn sight faster than Roy's computer.

He was glad of the interruption. "It's depressing looking at all those missing persons. How can there be quite so many o' them?"

"Sad reflection of our time. I'm haunted by them and the thought they could go from missing to murdered."

"Aye. You'd a question for me."

"I sure do." Shona leaned back in her chair. "You're my Dundee guru. Are Scott McLuskey and our Margaret related?"

He was silent.

Shona gave him time to think.

"I think Scott might be her nephew. If it's the same laddie he's a wee bit on the wild side."

She handed over the three names. "You're best shot. Apart from Scott, what have this lot been up to?"

He scrutinised the paper and handed it back. "You'd be better looking it up. I'm no' quite in the loop having been off for so long."

She left him to resume his search.

Well, well, The Battleship McLuskey and Scott are related. Must be through marriage. Still, an interesting spin, having a criminal in the family. Must go down a treat with the Runcie side.

The lad in Perth Prison was in the first few weeks of a two-year sentence for assault to serious injury. GBH as it was called when she worked in Oxford. Beat his girlfriend to a pulp and she lost her baby. It left her wondering why he was only doing two years. She'd have given him twenty-five to life in Barlinnie. He'd be high on her suspect list if he had been loose when the murder happened.

Pearl, or whatever she was called, had an endless stream of petty theft, mainly shoplifting. It would appear she didn't believe in paying for any items she needed. Didn't sound like the sort of person to murder someone in a bothy. Still, you never knew. Her profile picture gave the distinct impression she'd be strong enough. An interview when she was ready.

That left Scott. She picked up the phone to ask Margaret a few questions. Turned out Scott, 'the wee wastrel', to quote Margaret, was indeed her nephew. No she wouldn't answer any questions about him. Ask his druggie mother.

"Trouble in McLuskey paradise." The humongous rubber plant on top of her filing cabinet indicated complete indifference to her words.

"I don't blame you. But it's fun knowing McLuskey has a thorn in the flesh.

She asked Iain and Abigail to bring Scott's mother in for a chat. The woman usually went to the chemist for a methadone prescription round about now so the pair were dispatched in the direction of Boots.

"No shopping in town. In, meet the mother, in the car and back."

It was best to be straight with Nina when it came to a shopping centre. She was likely to come back with the witness and six shopping bags full of designer clothes and shoes. She managed to do this in the time it would take most people to heat a microwave meal.

"You're no fun, Shona."

"And your fun levels are off the stratosphere." Her smile took the sting from her words.

Peter knocked on her door. "I've an answer on our boy in the Eastern."

Jason clattering through the door, closely followed by Abigail, interrupted his revelation.

"You'll never guess what's happened, Ma'am."

31

He thought about his upcoming job. The clear nights and crisp skies made it more difficult. Rain, fog, cloud cover, all those were his friends. Long summer nights one of the enemies, as were the marks. Marks were studied carefully. The weather was studied carefully. Nothing could be done about the weather. Victims were another matter.

Preparation was key to getting it right. To not getting caught. A competent disguise was also a tool of his trade. A false moustache, a slight stoop, a wig with long wavy hair instead of a short style made all the difference.

Excitement levels rose at the thought of what lay ahead. His sexual arousal was strong, but forced back down. Later was the time for such things. Control of emotions, of feelings, of the body was everything. This had been learnt during childhood. Control yourself, make no sound, and don't let them know how you really feel. Keep out of the way.

The current lust for killing had also been developed in childhood. A release from the torment, it started small. A bird lured with tempting titbits. Time taken until the Little Bustard was tame enough to catch and kill. Patience learned and developed over months and years. Then larger animals followed, cats, dogs, and horses until, at last, the first human. It was almost a spiritual experience. A religion known only to a select few, those who chose to kill for pleasure. Who released their tension by removing another life.

The time arrived, the streets deadly quiet, just as he liked it. Streets that he knew well. He did not know most of his victims. However, this was a prearranged meeting. One of many, all of which ended in a business arrangement, with money changing hands. No money would be involved tonight.

The meeting place was the top of the law hill. No CCTV camera's here. Given the amount of murders that had happened in this place, that was not a wise move. No lights other than the red warning beacon at the top of the TV mast. They huddled in the shadow of the war memorial. No one around, it was still better to be sure.

"What have you got for me?" The grey haired woman leaned in closer. He could smell fresh peppermint on her breath. The woman kept herself beautiful. Spent money holding back the ravages of time. This person had been kind to her. Saw something special in her, hence her loyalty was unwavering. The large amounts of large value notes involved, also sealed the loyalty.

This woman had been carefully researched and pursued. Lonely, with not much of a life, her friends all married, she was left on the shelf, and dropped from their social calendars. No family to speak of. Not one solitary person in her life to worry about or to love her. She was fruit ripe for the picking. It did not take much to strike up a casual friendship that deepened and grew. Or so she thought.

Patience was always of value. Nothing happened by chance. Everything carried out with evil and determined precision, nothing in this life was ever wasted.

"This assignment is extra special."

She giggled. A sound usually heard from teens it sounded strange from this woman's lips. Sounded strange in this place at this time.

"Anything. You know I will do anything."

"You have proven this. Always. Let us go. We cannot discuss this here."

The woman followed him to the car. No hesitation. She trusted this man, the only one to show her any kindness.

If she could tell her future she would flee into the night.

This special assignment was murder.

32

"Do come in."

"Sorry, Ma'am. You really won't believe this though," said Abigail.

"Are you going to tell us, or keep us in suspense?"

"The council divvied up the info without murmur. All keys are present and correct."

"Hardly revolutionary information."

Shona opened her mouth to continue when the phone rang.

"I'll see all of you in the briefing room when I'm done."

"It's Mary."

"Hi yourself."

"No time for niceties. I had a quick look at the young lad who came in earlier today. He'd had his throat cut, but not sure if that was anti or post mortem."

"Good point."

"The real reason I'm ringing. I examined him to see if he was raped post mortem. The answer is yes."

"Same pattern then. Semen?"

"No. Your killer, or rapist, if they are not one and the same, used a condom. The Jury's still out on whether this was rape by a human or an implement was used."

"This case gets more revolting by the minute."

"Unfortunately, I've seen more than my fair share of degradation in my time."

"I'm beginning to have the same experience. Sometimes my job is too much to bear."

"The fact we're bringing the killers to justice keeps

us going."

The team were ready and waiting. She updated them on Mary's initial findings.

"That's so sick," said Jason.

"I take it you mean evil rather than good." Modern slang had Shona confused on a daily basis.

"Of course I do, Ma'am. We need to catch this bastard."

"Language." Shona's mild tone indicated she felt the same.

"Sorry, Ma'am, but you've got to agree this is deranged."

"This killer isn't right in the head." The situation had the rare effect of making sure Roy and Jason were on the same page.

The briefing room was not to be. The druggie mother was now in residence in the station. They knew this from the amount of shouted expletives which rang out loud and clear.

"Keep your language clean."

"Who the fu—?"

"Shut up." Shona's fist slamming off the table shocked the woman into obeying.

Even through the ravages of drug use it was apparent she had once been beautiful. Her voice, apart from the swearing, indicated she came from the upper echelons of Dundee society. That would tally with her being related to the battleship McLuskey.

"I am going to speak to you nicely, and I want you to return the favour."

Mrs McLuskey glared at her, arms crossed. Her pose said one wrong move and your dead.

Shona's relaxed pose indicated, 'I'm trying to be nice to you here'. Her thoughts said, *remember her son's missing. You cannot smack her around the head.*

"Mrs McLuskey, your son hasn't been seen for a few weeks. Do you know where he is?"

"I don't keep fu..." She took in the look on Shona's face, "Tabs on him. He can look after himself. He's a big boy now and doesn't need mummy's apron strings to hang on to."

Fairly eloquent for someone who'd just had methadone.

"We really need to speak to him, Mrs McLuskey. Are you able to tell us where he might hang out?"

"Do I hell. Do I look like someone who gives a fu—?"

"I fully understand. Do you have the names of any of his friends?" Shona decided getting into an argument with the woman wasn't going to help their cause. She did, however, plan on having a word with uniform. They could follow her and find her dealer. This woman was on more than methadone and Shona planned on cutting her supply off at the pass.

"Last I heard he was mucking about with Mark Insley and Johnny Parr."

"Thank you, Mrs McLuskey. You've been very helpful. Give my regards to Margaret."

The woman scowled at her. "That shi—"

Shona leaned over the table and said, her voice low, "I've been polite up until now. One more expletive out of that foul mouth of yours and I will arrest you. Now get out of my station and I hope I never see you again."

It was a relief to be back with the team. They were knee deep in discussion and Abigail was adding info to the boards. Shona had to admit; turning the room into one large whiteboard was inspired. She pulled back a chair and sat down. Following her last disaster with the chair she did it carefully.

"Abigail what did you have for us?"

"Six people had access to the spare keys for the cemetery."

"That's not many for a place the size of the council."

"Nope. All the keys are present and accounted for. The key holders, on the other hand, are not."

"What?"

"One Lesley King is AWOL and has been for weeks. Hasn't turned up for work once."

"Strange. You'd think if she'd absconded she'd have taken one of the keys."

"Unless she got a duplicate."

"Good point. Let's pin Lesley down." Shona focussed on Peter. "You had something momentous—"

"I'm sorry to interrupt, Ma'am, but I hadn't finished."

"Hurry up then."

"The mystery of the shut down CCTV cameras."

"Fire away."

"Twenty three people could get into the CCTV. Currently one of those, Nadia Badowski, is also on the AWOL list."

"Curiouser and curiouser, said Alice"

"Ma'am, if you dinnae mind me saying. It's always curious with you involved."

"It certainly is. Now, who do you think our young lad in the grave is?"

"Looks like it could be Tommy McShane."

"Details."

"Twenty one years old. Sole guardian for his wee brother. Neighbours called it in when they heard the wean crying and shouting for help." He stopped and cleared his throat.

"Not good." Shona gave the sergeant time to

compose himself. Kids in trouble always melted Peter's heart.

"He'd been on his own for three days."

"Where is he now?"

"In foster care."

"What do we know about Tommy?"

"Not much. Someone in Uniform caught him soliciting once. Sent him packing with a ticking off and told him to get a proper job."

"We'll visit his neighbours in the morning. You lot pack up and go home. I'm off for dinner with the Chief Constable."

"How the other half live."

"Nina, you can go in my place. His train's delayed by two hours so he's going to be in a foul mood. As will the Chief."

"Thanks, but nah. Someone of my pay grade shouldn't be worrying about such things."

"I thought not."

The dinner was interesting. As Shona thought neither of her companions was swinging from the chandeliers. However, they remained polite and courteous, which is about the best she could hope for. The big boss wanted an update, which she gave in thorough detail.

"For a small City, Dundee seems to have more than its fair share of serial killers."

"I couldn't agree more, Sir. I'd like a few less."

"There won't be anyone left in Dundee to kill soon. Everyone will leave." The Chief Constable put down his knife and fork and leaned back in his chair.

"Quite the opposite," said the Chief. "The population is growing. Dundee is an up and coming city."

I wish I was up and leaving. There's only so much of this a girl can take. She thought longingly of a

Talisker and asked for another designer fizzy water.

"Did you call the press briefing?"

"I did, Sir. All set up for 9 a.m. as you requested."

"Who will be there? I would like to be prepared."

"Who *won't* be there, Sir? The jungle drums were busy and most of the usual players had already heard. *The BBC* and *STV* news are also joining us." She paused and scowled. "As will *The Courier.*"

"That paper seems to buzz around us like wasps. Haven't they got better things to do, like report on the fiscal failings of the council?" Thomas's scowl was deeper than Shona's. His bushy eyebrows, in direct contrast to his bald head, met in the middle.

"Apparently not, Sir."

Douglas's mother was still in shingles hell and he hadn't found anyone else to palm the kids off on. So, he was currently at the cinema, leaving Shona home alone. Shakespeare still hadn't forgiven her for the breakfast fiasco and was currently sulking on the top of an antique dresser, tail hanging down and twitching. Shona ignored her, curled up on the Sofa and phoned her mother. An hour of soothing chatter ensued. The antics of the neighbours in a so-called peaceful English village had her laughing out loud. Somewhere in the midst of it Shakespeare got over her strop and came to join her on the sofa.

33

The press briefing appeared chaotic but, was anything but. Held outside, the usual sticky beakers were gathered at the back listening to everything that was being said. The Chief Constable remained professional and calm answering all questions clearly but without giving one iota of valuable information away.

"Simon Cardington from the *BBC*. What would you say to those who feel that the police are not in control in Dundee?"

"I would say they need to look at their own affairs before criticizing Police Scotland. Criminals and murderers will do what they do. It is our job to catch them."

"Zoe McIntosh, *Scottish Herald*. What are you doing to catch them? Nothing it would seem."

"This case is being handled in a professional manner. The officer in charge is following a number of lines of enquiry. One of these is to ask the public for their assistance. If anyone knows, or sees, anything which could help with this case call the Chief Investigation Officer, Detective Inspector McKenzie on 0300 572 8761."

"Adanna Okofor, *Dundee Courier*. It would appear that no one is guarding the cemeteries around the area. One would think this would be top priority to catch the killer."

Shona took a deep breath. *You stupid cow. Put that in the press and it will tip the killer off to use other body dumps.* She made a mental note to grab her nemesis and have a strong word with her.

"I'm sure you'll appreciate we cannot share any

details of how we are investigating this case. That will be all."

Shona left with a feeling that she'd like to kick Adanna right up her pert backside.

"Lets' go and interrogate Tommy's neighbours. There's only so much I can take."

Peter put down *The Courier* and stood up.

"Is Colin the Clown in there?" she asked.

"Not that I've seen. Not looked at the online version yet, though."

"My you've gone all high tech. At least they've kept his identity quiet. There aren't many clowns wandering around Dundee."

Moving over to Nina's desk she asked her to divyy up the remainder of the team and try to find something out about the missing Lesley King and Nadia Badowski.

Tommy lived in what looked like a squat. The building had fallen into disrepair. That was the kindest thing that could be said about it. At first glance it looked like his neighbours had fallen into disrepair as well. Most of them were high on drugs, drink or both.

"Did you smell weed growing in that last place?" Peter kept his voice low.

"I surely did. Tip off uniform once we're finished."

After knocking on several doors they came up trumps. This door was as battered as the rest, but the inside told a different story. The door opened onto a spacious open plan area. It was sparsely furnished, but clean and brightly painted. Comfy sofa's covered in multicolured throws made the place look welcoming. A woman of about forty stood in the door. She held the hand of a two year old.

Shona showed her ID and gave their names.

"Please, come in." She led them inside and popped the child in a playpen. He picked up a lorry and ran it up and down making vrooming noises.

"Blaze Derbyshire. Can I get you a cold drink?" Her accent was cut glass English.

They settled on coke and Blaze headed for the kitchen.

"Why would someone like this be living here? That accent says she's from the Home Counties."

"I've nae clue, Ma'am. A wee bitty odd if you ask me. Maybe she's the dealer."

Unfortunately his voice was a higher than it should have been and the returning Blaze heard him. She laughed.

"An easy mistake to make. I'm not a dealer; I'm from the new church plant that's just been planted here, New Fire Dundee."

"Why would that bring you here? I don't mean to Dundee, I mean living in this du… building?"

"It does look like a dump. That's the reason we're here. We believe in living with the people we reach out to. Show God's love by getting alongside those who live on the outskirts of humanity."

Pay dirt. She'll know everyone well.

"Did you know, Tommy McShane?"

"Absolutely. I spent a lot of time with him and his little brother, Charlie."

"What can you tell us about them?"

"I can tell you that boy loved Charlie and would do anything to protect him. There's no way he would deliberately go off and leave him."

Shona showed her an airbrushed photo of their corpse. "Is this him?"

"Yes, that's Tommy." Something clicked in her head. "Goodness, he's dead isn't he."

122

"We think so."

"That poor boy. I'll be praying for his soul. I'll also pray for Charlie."

"I'll pray for his soul as well," said Peter, a staunch Catholic.

Shona felt like she was in the middle of one of her mother's church services. It was time to get them back on track. "Tell us about Tommy?"

"A nice lad. Kind and gentle. Looked after his brother well." She hesitated.

"If there's anything we need to know about it. It could help us catch his killer."

"He lost his job and was terrified they'd take Charlie away. He turned a trick or two to supplement Job Seekers."

Shona thought the phrase sounded odd coming from this woman's lips.

"I gave him food when I could, but we aren't well off either."

She took in Shona's disbelieving look.

"I know my accent says I've pots of money. My husband and I turned our backs on it all when we decided to become missionaries. Both sides struck us out of their wills."

"Very noble of you. What are the neighbours round about like?"

The woman gazed at them and said nothing.

"This is a murder investigation."

"I can assure you none of them murdered Tommy."

"How can you be so sure?"

She hesitated, then, "Most of them skirt around the edges of what might be considered legal. But none of them are capable of murder."

"We need to be the judge of that."

The woman's eyes narrowed. "I was a lawyer before I gave up the rat race. You may not want to pursue this."

"That sounded like a threat to me." Shona looked to Peter. "Did it sound like a threat to you?"

"It certainly did, Ma'am."

"One more threat and I'll arrest you. I assume your law degree came from Oxford or Cambridge?"

"Of course."

"Well, you're not a particularly bright lawyer if you don't realise it's not worth the paper it's written on up here."

"What do you mean?"

"Are you deliberately being thick? We have a different legal system. You're not qualified to practice."

"I knew that."

"Pleased to hear it. Now, your neighbours. What are they like?"

"Perfectly pleasant human beings. Delightful actually."

"Was it you who reported Tommy missing?"

"It was. I heard Charlie and called the local constabulary."

"Did he say anything about his brother?"

"He was too busy having a meltdown."

"Get on to uniform and get this lot in. If they skirt around the edges of the law, as she so delicately put it, I'm sure they're a bunch of criminals."

"Are you mental? If you don't mind me asking that is."

"Why? What gives you that impression?"

"We'll be interviewing this lot until our dying day. Nothing useful will come out of their mouths."

"Get them in anyway. You never know what we'll be able to shake out of them."

34

It took about fifty seconds for Shona to work out that Peter was right. Wasn't he always when it came to the good citizens of Dundee? They were currently slobbing around in the waiting room. It looked like the start of a rehab course. She took a deep breath and swallowed several mouthfuls of scalding coffee. A couple of Kit Katss stood in for lunch. *Not exactly a balanced diet but heck, needs must. And Kit Kats had milk in so that made them nutritious.*

She headed to the interview room via the main office. Everyone was missing except Abigail.

"Get on to social services and find out what they know about Tommy and his brother."

"Righty ho."

"Where are the rest hiding?"

"Canteen. They're dying of malnutrition or something."

"The only people dying of starvation round here are Peter and I. We also seem to be the only ones working."

"Excuse me. I'm busy making phone calls. I've not had a morsel to eat either."

Shona pulled a spare Kit Kat from her pocket and lobbed it at her sergeant. "Here."

Abigail pulled back the wrapper and bit off a huge chunk."

"Ttnk. Yr a sayer."

"I'll take it your pleased?"

Abigail nodded in response.

First up was Kayne Macintosh, all six, tattooed, feet of him. If there was an inch of him without ink Shona did not want to see it.

"Mr. Macintosh."

His glazed eyes wandered the room.

"Mr Macintosh."

With a valiant effort he focussed on Shona.

"You speaking tae me?"

"Of course I'm speaking to you. Who else is there?"

"Him." his hand shook as he pointed at Peter.

"Might be better if I took over, Ma'am."

"Feel free. I feel like banging my head on the desk. Or his head."

"You don't want to be doing that." He turned to their witness. "Kayne, listen tae me. Answer a few questions and you can go home to your weans."

"What's up with her? I've no' done nothing."

"Nobody's saying you have. Did you know Tommy?"

"Everybody knew Tommy, and his wee laddie."

"Did you ever see any o' his pals."

"Keep myself to myself like. Dinnae poke my nose into anyone's business."

"Very civic minded of you," Shona chipped in.

"What's she on aboot?"

Peter turned to Shona and whispered in her ear. "Might be better if you left me to this. Send in Jason."

With a sigh, Shona stood up and hurried off to find Jason. *I'm reduced to running errands. How the mighty have fallen.*

Abigail hadn't managed to get the right person at Social Services so was waiting for them to get back to her.

"What's the status of our two missing council workers?'

"Not much yet. We're still working on it."

"You carry on and I'll see if I can get hold of the

right social worker."

Before she had a chance to pick up the phone she was called into the chief's office.

"I've had Ex Lord Provost Brown on the phone."

"Pa Broon? What could he possibly want?"

"What have I told you about respect, Shona?" A smile fought its way through. He bravely held it off.

"Respect where respect's due, Sir. Message received loud and clear."

"Pa, I mean Ex Lord Provost Brown wants to know why you arrested his tenants?"

"Is he addled? I haven't arrested any..." Realisation dawned. "Are you telling me that Pa Broon is the landlord for that slum?"

"Shona! I will not tell you again."

"Sir, his tenants are currently waiting to be interviewed as witnesses. Every last one of them is a drunk or a drug addict."

"Our esteemed Lord Provost cannot be held responsible for the lifestyle choices of his tenants. I will inform him that they have merely been asked to assist with our enquiries. That will be all."

"Sir, I think his property may be a death trap."

"Please do inform the relevant authorities."

She didn't bother saying anything else. As per, he wasn't listening anyway.

The social work department was helpful in the extreme. Yes, they knew the family, but Tommy looked after his younger brother well. The boy was fed, clean and attended school regularly. Charlie was quiet, polite, and a little on the thin side.

"Where is he at the moment?"

"With his foster parents."

"Can I have their name and address as we will need to interview the boy?"

"Of course. Nehemiah and Blaze Derbyshire. The same address as Tommy but flat 2b."

Why didn't she mention this when we were there? Strange all round.

35

She asked Blaze to bring Charlie in. Couldn't be done. He was currently at church summer school, which was residential, but she would do so after that. He'd had enough disruption in his life. She wanted to give him this one thing before his life broke apart once more.

"Should I tell him about his brother's death?"

"Could you wait until we've spoken to him? Then you can tell him here."

"Of course. Anything to assist the police."

Shona was trying to work out where they were going with the case. She'd come up with the cube root of nothing when a whirlwind and a large puppy flew through the door. The puppy jumped onto her lap and set to, slapping her in the face with its tail. The other end got busy rearranging things on her desk. Just to make things really complicated, the King Charles Spaniel was also called Charlie. She grabbed him and popped him on the floor. He didn't take this lightly and occupied himself trying to get up again. Her tickling him behind the ear stopped the rucus.

"Shona, we haven't seen you in like ages." The speaker was blonde haired, blue eyed, seven years old and wearing a pink and white flowery dress. This was Douglas's daughter, Alice.

"It has been rather a long time. What brought you to Bell Street?"

"Not what silly. Who brought me? Daddy did. We walked." The urchin flew around the desk and threw her arms around Shona's neck.

"Where is Daddy?" Shona mumbled through a mouthful of silky hair.

"Speaking to some boring man."

Out of the mouth of babes. Douglas would have to be warned about his daughter's penchant for repeating things verbatim.

"How was the cruise?"

"Fablis. We had ice cream every day and went swimming."

Obviously the delights of the Mediterranean islands passed the youngster by.

"You and daddy weren't there, Shona. Me and Rory wanted you there."

"Where is Rory?" This was her big brother, now the advanced age of thirteen.

"He's gone fishing with his friend. Yuck. That's horrible for those fishes, Shona."

"Let's go and find you a drink and a cake."

The girl skipped alongside her, chattering all the while. The puppy followed beside them, tail wagging. It provided a refreshing breeze of air in the sweltering atmosphere. They found a couple of strawberry tarts in the kitchen and chewed in companionable silence. The puppy did it's best to beg bits of the tart. It had to make do with the occasional crumb that dropped to the floor.

Alice broke the quietness. "Are you and daddy going to get married?"

A piece of pastry went down the wrong way and Shona coughed and spluttered. Abigail heard the racket and came rushing in. She slapped Shona on the back.

The puppy leapt around barking fit to awaken the dead.

Alice hopped from foot to foot. "Shona. Are you going to die?" She promptly burst into tears.

"No." Splutter, cough. cough. "No one's..."

Cough, cough, cough. "Dying."

She took a few sips of the water and wiped her face of the tears. "Come here, sweetie." She crouched down and pulled the wee lass into a hug. "I'm okay."

Douglas entered the kitchen, which was now overcrowded. Cupboard would be a more appropriate term than kitchen.

"What's going on?"

"I need a word with you." She glanced at Abigail. "Could you take Alice to see Uncle Peter?"

The sergeant led off the blue-eyed truth machine.

Shona updated Douglas on what had gone down. "You need to watch your mouth around Alice. She's listening to everything."

He stopped laughing long enough to say, "I don't know where she got that marriage bit from. The day I want to propose you'll be the first person I will inform, not my kids."

"She had been chattering about her friend being a bridesmaid because her mum's getting married again."

"Ah. That explains it. She's into frocks at the moment. Wants me to buy her some frilly number that costs about a hundred pounds and is totally impractical."

"She's a mercenary wee tyke. Trying to get us hitched just so she can get all dolled up."

"She's her mother's daughter in more ways than one."

36

Once Uncle Peter had finished with Alice, he presented himself in Shona's office.

"That wee bairn is a great antidote for the shower I've just interviewed."

"Watch what you say in front of her. She's repeating everything verbatim."

"More than you can say about our witnesses. Barely a coherent thought amongst them."

"Did you beat it out of them?"

"Almost. I was tempted to get my dear departed daddy's truncheon out." He took in the look on Shona's face and added, "I restrained myself."

"So a total dud then?"

"Not quite. One juicy titbit came up a couple of times." He paused and gazed at Shona. A wicked glint brightened his eyes.

"Spit it out or I swear you're on traffic 'til the day you die."

"That'd be sooner, rather than later ,on traffic."

"Peter!"

"Oor Ruskies came to visit a few times."

"The Kalashnakov twins?" She sat open mouthed, picked up her water bottle, unscrewed the cap and took several gulps. "Stephan, Gregor and Pa Broon. Our merry little band together again."

"What's he got to do with it? Don't tell me he's on the scene as well."

"As I live and breathe. Large as life and six times as evil."

"Are we ever going to be free of them?"

"Probably not." she picked up a pen. The clicking

of the top being depressed accompanied her next words. "Pa Broon owns the building that Tommy lived in."

"That pen's no' Pa Broon You're going to break it."

She put the pen back.

Peter continued. "I might have known that hovel belonged to the ex Lord Provost. He'd do anything to save a couple of bob."

"Whilst screwing the occupants." At Peter's raised eyebrow she added. "Out of their money. I meant out of their money."

"To be honest both versions would probably stand up in court."

"Let's pay the brothers Grimm a visit."

Before they got out of the door, Roy grabbed her.

"I've dredged up some more info on Cara's boyfriend."

"Great stuff. Can it wait until our return? We've a couple of Russian thugs to annoy."

"Might be worth hearing before you go."

"Hang on." She grabbed Jason and Iain. "Bring the Alexeyevs in."

"On our own? They'll kill us."

"What? You—"

"No arguing." She yelled over to Abigail. "Go with this pair of big girl's blouses to grab the Russian Twins."

"Three of us? We—"

"For heavens sake. What are you lot doing in CID? You should be rescuing cats from trees. Nina, go with them."

"Can we take guns?"

"No you flaming well can't. Go and get them here. use you initiative, and some muscle. Now move it. "

They took drinks through to the briefing room, having decided the ban was on hold again.

"That's not tea. It's industrial strength pipe cleaner."

Peter smacked his lips. "Just the way I like it."

"Our man Barry's in deep shi... trouble," said Roy.

Shona leaned forward. "Dish."

"Up to his Welsh ears in debt."

"That doesn't make him a murderer."

"Being in cahoots with Sal McLintosh, in order to get out of that debt, might though."

"Who's he?"

Peter enlightened her. "She," he stressed the word, "Is the matriarch of Scotland's oldest crime family. She makes the Alexeyevs look like a pair of pussies."

"How come we've never crossed paths with her before?"

"Because she's stuck to Glasgow, Edinburgh and Aberdeen up until now. She's a big player, so Dundee's beneath her," said Peter.

"Word on the street is that she's got over her prejudice," said Roy. "She's muscling in."

"Oor Ruskies won't like that."

"Why me? I'm applying to go back to Oxford."

37

The team returned without the brothers. Why was Shona not surprised? This was a regular occurrence when it came to bringing in the Bobbsey Twins.

"Seriously? You're meant to be a crack team. Why can't you crack on and arrest a couple of thugs?"

"They refused to come," said Nina.

"Threw us out," added Iain.

"Physically. I think they've broken my arm." Jason's arm did look bruised. He was the most accident-prone bloke in the whole of Police Scotland.

"There's no swelling. The bruise will make you look like a big boy. The rest of you just look like a bunch of pansies." She added. "Peter, Roy, come with me. We're off to arrest Bill and Ben for assaulting a police officer."

This time they took handcuffs, a couple of huge Alsatians, and their burly handlers.

"This ought to help take the wind out their sails."

"Those dogs are taking the wind out of mine. They're as big as Gorillas," said Roy. He was staying a wary few feet away from them.

"You're not frightened of a couple of wee puppies?" She put her hand out and the 'puppies' growled and bared razor sharp teeth. She yanked her hand back quicker than a striking guard dog. "Maybe you're right."

The handlers and the puppies sat in the back of the van. They'd already called some uniform to be around the back entrance in case Alexeyev 1 and 2 made a bolt for it.

"You cannot bring those animals into our club. It is against health and safety."

"I never thought,you pair would be bothered with such things as health and safety. You're the biggest health and safety hazard Dundee has to cope with."

"You are always disrespectful to us," said Stephan. Gregor's only role in the proceedings seemed to be standing around glowering at Shona. He did it with aplomb.

"Your face is going to stick like that," said Shona.

"We'd like you to accompany us to the station, " said Roy.

"We will not do this." Stephan bolted with Gregor hot on his heels.

Leads unclipped and one word from their handler was the cue for the dogs to take off after them. The club shook with the force of the twins shouting and the dog's barking.

"We need ear defenders," said Roy.

"We need compensation for having to put up with Dundee's answer to the mafia."

"You're telling me."

"Peter, guard the door. Roy, this is your chance to show me what you're made of. We need to go handcuff Tweedledum and Tweedledee."

Shona and Roy joined the chase. Punters scattered with most heading for the door. Several of the dancers headed in that direction as well. Where they thought they were going wearing nothing but a thong, Shona didn't want to think about. Peter, enjoying his job as always, stopped them there. Thuds and screams were heard as the Alsatians assisted the suspects to the floor. Shona and Roy caught up and pulled out handcuffs. Hands yanked behind their backs the twins were soon cuffed and sitting on chairs.

The dogs, Darcy and Mali, played their part

beautifully. They had the menacing growls off to a fine art and this kept their suspects in line.

"Add resisting arrest to your rap sheet."

"It's list of offences here, Ma'am."

"I know that but it always sounds Gucci on the telly. I've always wanted to say it."

"You can be weird at times."

"Peter, my man, have you only just worked that one out?"

Peter just shook his head. "It's one big adventure working with you."

"Laugh a minute. Well it is when we get to play with this pair."

"Stephan and Gregor Alexeyev, I am arresting you for assaulting a police officer and resisting arrest."

The handcuffed twins were thrown into the back of the van. The dogs did not take their eyes off them for the whole journey, and escorted them all the way to the interview room. The dogs left and Gregor was dragged off to a cell screaming fit to burst eardrums.

"Give him a sedative. It might shut him up."

"It's no' legal, Ma'am."

"A woman can dream."

The minute the dogs left Stephan resorted to his usual revolting self.

"You must let us go. You persecute us. Always, for no reason."

"We had plenty reason. You assaulted several police officers."

"This is not true. If you keep us here you will regret it."

Shona got up so close and personal with Stephan, she could almost see his tonsils. "Now you're threatening a police officer. If I were you I'd keep my trap shut."

"You will regret this."

"So you keep saying. It's getting boring."

"Why have you brought us here?"

"Are you thick or what? I told you why you'd been arrested but I'll repeat it again." She proceeded to do so.

"The officer fell whilst I was assisting him out of the door. I helped him up. No more. No assault."

There was a knock at the door and in walked Margaret McLuskey. Wearing her customary grey suit she looked like a battleship in full sail. With a chest that could double as a shelf on which to sit your coffee, she was a formidable sight. She was also the twins' lawyer.

"Margaret, how nice to see you."

"Cut the sarcasm."

"I thought I was being particularly nice. Did the jungle drums alert you to your clients' incarceration?"

Margaret snorted. "Why are you always so rude?"

Using her usual tactics with the woman Shona ignored her question. "Your client's were asked to come down to the station and answer a few questions. They started a fight and one of my officer's was injured. Pretty clear cut."

"I told you, the gentleman got injured accidently. You do not listen, or you are an idiot."

Shona opened her mouth.

Margaret cut her off at the pass. "I would like a word with my client alone."

Shona shut down the recording and left them to it.

"Annie, I need food and I need it fast."

Annie, the patron saint of canteen food, shoved a plate of macaroni cheese over the counter.

Shona shovelled it in like her last meal and dashed back to the interview room. "I'll pay you later," she threw over her shoulder.

"On the house. You're fading away."

"My client states there is video evidence regarding your officer's injuries. You are free to look at this any time."

Shona's look could kill an elephant six miles away. "Very magnanimous of you both."

"He is also willing to answer all your questions, fully and honestly."

"Are you having a laugh? He doesn't know the meaning of honest."

"DI McKenzie—"

"I know, you're going to report me." Shona's tone was weary. "Let's put that aside and concentrate on the questions."

The questions elicited nothing. Yes, they'd visited the young man. He was behind with his rent. They'd been asked by the Ex Lord Provost to visit and discuss the options for paying.

"Did that include murder? Best way to get him out of the flat."

"Are you accusing my client of murder?"

"Even you should be able to work out it was a question, not an accusation."

The questions went on and on with nothing to show for it. In the end the twins were kept under lock and key until the CCTV at Cat's Eyes was produced.

38

"We need to speak to Sal McLintosh."

There was stunned silence. After what seemed like hours, but was probably a matter of seconds, p

Peter said, "Best get Glasgow to do that."

"Why would we do that?"

"Seriously, Ma'am. Trust me on this one. Glasgow has the expertise here."

It wasn't often Peter went against what she had to say. She considered it for a minute then decided to go with his instinct. When it came to policing Scotland he knew what he was doing. "Fine. You can arrange it."

"Roy, go and get the security camera footage from Cat's Eyes."

"With pleasure, Ma'am." The gleam in his eye said the ex girlfriend was relegated to the pages of history. Roy was back in the game.

God help us, thought Shona. Wild isn't the word for it when he's foot loose and fancy free.

"Has anyone managed to work out what our victims had in common?"

"They're all blonde, Ma'am," said Jason.

"Good point, but I'm not sure what relevance this has. Anything else?"

" A couple of them are linked to Cat's Eyes."

"They are." She thought for a moment, the said, "It's not likely the twins would bump off their own dancers. Especially not one as popular as Raven."

"Word on the street is their takings have taken a nosedive since that wee lassie died," said Peter.

"Proves my point. The twins might be my thorn in the flesh, but they take the making of money seriously to the point of obsession."

"What's the skinny on our two missing council workers?"

Nina said, "I took Lesley King. Fifty-two years old. Worked for the council all her life. Spinster of this parish. Keeps herself to herself and doesn't appear to have many friends. Quiet type. Her colleagues didn't know much about her. Her only living relative seems to be a distant cousin. She had phone calls from her occasionally."

"Get her phone records."

"My next job."

Abigail took over. "Nadia Badowski. Young mum of a three year old. Reliable to a fault, and never missed a day until she disappeared. Husband is beside himself with worry. He's been storming the doors of the station every day. He said she loved her son to distraction and wouldn't go off without him."

"There has to be something going on. I smell a whole plague of rats, never mind one. They were up to something suspicious."

"And I'd say they paid the ultimate price," said Nina.

"I wouldn't take the odds on you being right. Get Nadia's phone records as well, and both their bank details."

"Consider it done."

"What colour hair have that pair got. Nina looked at her notes. "Brown for Nadia."

"Grey for Lesley."

"What colour was she before she went grey?"

"Not sure, I'll find out."

Shona trawled through HOLMES looking for similar cases. The nearest she got was some nutjobs who were recreating Burke and Hare. With live victims."

She picked up the phone and rang Birmingham CID. Introductions over she explained her case. "You had something similar."

"Our boys can't be your perpetrator. They're currently serving life without parole in Wakefield."

"Are they regularly in touch with anyone? Could they be doing it by remote control so to speak?"

"It's a possibility. I'll try to find out for you. What's your number?"

She handed it over and hung up.

She'd no sooner put it down than it rang, startling her.

"DI McKenzie."

.

39

Four Weeks Previously

The park was the perfect place to meet someone in secret. Four hundred vast acres of lawns, play parks, a zoo, and more importantly, dense woodland. The woods provided textbook cover. No one traipsed through the clinging foliage during the day. Definitely not at night. The night was left to woodland animals - foxes, badgers, voles and hedgehogs. To the creeping vegetation which, in summer took over this area.

Despite the lateness of the hour the woman was bright, perky. Her husband completely unaware of what she was up to. He had no clue how she was supplementing their income. His job in a supermarket and her job at the council did not support the lifestyle they enjoyed. He thought she was merely careful with money. She loved him with a dazzling passion, but he wasn't the brightest Zarowska in the box. That suited her because she took control in this relationship.

She'd slipped a little something extra into his vodka tonight. He was snoring like a babushka, their son in the cot next to him. She put a hand on her stomach and stroked it gently. The baby growing inside her would need more room.

"I can't wait to meet you little one," she murmured.

A crashing in the undergrowth startled her. A magnificently antlered stag screamed to a stop just feet from her. She held her breath. If it charged this would be the end of her and the new life inside her. The animal stared for a few moments and then, with one nod of it's proud head, ran in off into the woods. The woman's pounding heart slowed.

Initially calm, her nervesnous grew the longer she waited. When would her business associate arrive? Usually punctual, this unusual occurrence had her rattled. She needed this final payment. It would secure their new home, one big enough for a growing family. No more crowding in one small room. She could almost touch the home. The musty smell of the undergrowth faded and was replaced by the scent of wild flowers. Freshly picked and arranged in a vase to decorate their sitting room. Her baby in a Moses basket, her toddler playing on the rug. Her sipping Polish tea.

The man watched from the thick cover of the trees. Imagining how this night would play out. Analysing every move. He took one step forward. Stopped. Listened. Nothing there, it was just a far too fertile imagination conjuring up demons. The lower branches of the tree touched his head. Pushed away, they snapped back into place immediately. He watched again. The plan was clarifying, becoming clearer with every passing second. He would enjoy this night. He would kill two birds with one stone. With that, he crept through the undergrowth with as much stealth as could be mustered.

Another trick learned in childhood, leading to him becoming a master of moving without making a sound. An important trick to acquire when planning on avoiding danger. It was equally as important when stalking a victim. This victim had been stalked for months before closing in. Then, a tentative approach, a burgeoning friendship and a girl with greed stamped through her. Of course, meticulous research guaranteed he already knew this. A deal was made. A deal with the devil.

She screamed and spun round at the hand on her shoulder.

"Hush." A hand was clamped over her mouth as someone whispered in her ear. "It is me. No need to worry. Quiet now."

"You scared me half to death."

"I am sorry. You were far away, not with me in this clearing. What were you thinking about my beautiful lady?"

"Just a dream. One you wouldn't understand."

"You should watch, not dream. These woods are dangerous."

"You'll protect me."

"Of course I will protect you."

"What have you got for me this time?"

"A very special assignment. You must come with me."

A smile lighting up her face, the woman followed.

He smiled inside as he led her to her fate. A fate predestined before their first meeting. This was meant to be. This was how her life was meant to end. The feeling of power, of control grew inside him like a living being. It consumed and brought release. Release from the boiling rage. Release from the tension. Release from the past and those who misused their power to abuse and ridicule. It brought release from the memories of a persistent barrage of blows and insults designed to grind a child down. To change the way they viewed life and to teach them to submit. This could either break them or forge a rod of steel, which ran right through the middle. This would make them stronger and allow them to survive. He chose the latter.

The balance had now shifted putting the power into the hands of the one who was once abused. No longer cringing but upright and strong, confident, and in charge. The bonds of the past had been broken.

She clambered into the luxury Bentley, the only car in an almost hidden car park. Settled into its leather seat, which enveloped her in exquisite luxury. She tugged on the seat belt, made sure it was tight. Safety paramount, she would find out it was a wasted concept. No seat belt would save her from what lay ahead. A contented sigh escaped from her lips. A powerful electric engine meant the car accelerated from 0 to 70 with barely a whisper. The roads in the park deserted there was no need to keep to the official speed. The gates lay open and the car shot through. The driver slowed on the roads, no need to attract unnecessary attention.

The woman settled back to enjoy the ride of her life. Or was it her death?

40

"Shona, its Bruce from Angus."

"I take it your not calling for a blether?"

"Nope. I've a case here I'd like to hand over to you."

"I've enough on my plate with my own cases. I don't mean to be rude but investigate your own."

"This *is* your case. It involves a crypt."

"The next words out of your mouth had better be 'I'm joking'."

"Afraid not. It's a bona fide crypt case, so it's all yours."

"Which cemetery?"

"Forfar Old Churchyard. Swimming with Crypts, so a perfect body dump for your man."

"Or woman."

She hung up and threw the phone at the wall. It chipped the plaster and dropped to the floor. Thankfully it remained in one piece.

"Give me a blasted break."

Neither version of a break was happening for her. Instead she was inside a car and on the way to Forfar.

"What's the deal with Mr Castanets?"

"His name's Alejandro."

Nina's inane chatter about her love life kept them going for the 30 minute journey to their destination.

Bruce met them, a fully suited, walking talking white ghost. "Thanks for coming. I'll introduce you to everyone and you can take charge of the case."

"I can't believe I'm doing your work as well as my own."

"Wish I could keep it, but protocol says I pass it on. It's part of your on-going investigation. Been a bit quiet round here recently so something to get my teeth into would be nice."

"We're Police Scotland now. One big happy family. I'm sure you could keep it."

"Shona, you and I both know, too many plods spoil the investigation." Bruce held his thumb and forefinger a couple of millimetres apart.

"Keep it tight. First rule we were taught."

The POLSA ushered her and Bruce through once she'd kitted up. He told her the local gravedigger had turned up to prepare a grave for a burial the next day. Dug his grave and had some time so decided to do a bit of a tidy up. Seemingly the gravediggers often did that in rural cemeteries.

"He noticed one of the crypts had been disturbed so called us."

This crypt was more like a small house than a grave. Grey, lichen covered and crumbling, the ravages of time had not treated it well. The doors stood open.

"Last burial here? I mean the crypt, not the cemetery."

"1865."

"That would explain its state. Can I go inside?"

He waved his arm in invitation.

She stopped at the doors and tried to move them. Solid. She managed about an inch.

"It took two of us to open them. Not much room so go alone."

Bent double she shuffled inside. It smelled of death, decay, mould and mildew. The body of a woman, perfectly presented in the death pose, took pride of place in the middle. She was lying on top of a stone coffin.

Given her state of decay Shona didn't think she had been there long. The pathologist would have the deciding say on that, but she'd hazard less than twenty-four hours.

She looked around, sweeping the area with her gaze. Methodically she covered every inch. Activating the voice memo on her phone she dictated her findings "Rain in the corner seeped in, maybe evidence if the killer went in that area." She gazed around again. The stone floor gave little away. "Maybe dirt from the killer's shoes? Check the shoes of all those with access today."

She backed out and sneezed several times.

"I'm glad you didn't do that in there."

Her white suit was now covered in green and black smears. There was small hole in the knee.

"I'd better change suits. This will look like DPM soon. Not the cleanest spot in the world."

Leaving the tent she passed Mary, who was entering.

"I didn't know this was your bailiwick."

"Everywhere is my bailiwick. I swear I'm the only pathologist in Scotland."

"You shouldn't be so good at your job."

The gravedigger was leaning on his spade at the entrance to the cemetery. A large man; despite his apparel of shorts and a t-shirt sweat poured down his face, which was florid. He was a walking, talking heart attack waiting to happen. He pulled a Crunchie from his pocket. Unwrapping it he stuffed it in his mouth and chewed.

Shona could almost hear his arteries furring. She flashed her ID. "Could you talk me through what you found?"

He swallowed, picked up a bottle of water and drank deeply. Then, wiping his mouth with the back of his hand, he was ready to talk. "I was doing a wee bitty tidying up. Wanted to keep the place spick and span, nice for tomorrows mourners."

"Very civic minded of you."

"It's bad enough burying someone without it looking a mess."

"The crypt?" Shona tapped her foot. *Will he ever get to the point?*

"Aye. I noticed the doors weren't quite shut. They should have been sealed tight."

"What did you do?"

"I thought the yobs from town had been in. Nothing better to do than vandalise graves."

"Has this happened before?"

"No, but they hang around in here drinking tinnies. They should bring back national service."

"Did you touch the grave?"

"Aye, I went to have a look inside. See if they'd done any damage."

"You've contaminated the crime scene, Mr...?"

"Lassiter. David Lassiter. An I didnae know it was a crime scene then."

"Did you open the doors any further?"

"Aye, a few inches. Then I shone the flashlight on my phone inside. Noticed yon woman and hot tailed it out of there. She's too fresh to be interred there."

"Iain, take Mr Lassiter to give a statement and swab him in every possible place. We'll need his shoes as well."

"What? What do you need my shoes for?"

"Evidence, Mr Lassiter. We'll give you a ride home."

"I came in my Ford Focus."

"You'll have no trouble getting home for a new pair then."

"Seriously, you lot are going to make me go home in my bare feet?"

"It's either that or the blue coveralls we wear on site. Take your pick."

Bare feet suddenly became much more appealing.

41

"We must stop meeting like this." The warm voice sent Shona's temperature soaring so high she felt her brain would explode.

"Douglas. Where are the kids?"

"My sister's carted them off to her caravan for a fortnight. Work and kids do not make for good bedfellows."

She smiled and moved on. "We've another corpse and another crypt used as a body dump."

"Your motto should be 'another day another murder'."

"Very witty. You should take up stand up."

"If it wasn't so public I'd kiss you right now. All this banter makes you look adorable."

"Why, Mr Lawson, I'm not that type of lady." This was said in a passable southern drawl.

"How many does that make now?"

"Four, although we're not sure Cara Ballieri is the same killer. Bothy's and crypts are a far cry from each other."

"They sure are. Talking of which, that bothy's still sealed off from the world. The rambling public of Scotland are braying for your blood. I'd like to open it again."

"Go for it. I was ready to release the crime scene anyway. I don't think there's anything more we can do."

Douglas spoke to the POLSA and Bruce and then bade her goodbye. He invited her out that night.

She responded by laughing. "In the middle of this? No chance my boy."

"It was worth a try".

She lightly touched his face. "It's always worth a try my love."

Passion deepened the colour in his eyes, as he walked away.

Shona watched him leave then hurried over to Bruce. "I take it there were shed loads of photos taken before I arrived."

"More than you can possibly imagine."

"Any chance of seeing them?"

"Your wish is my command. I'll get the memory card and we can use my computer. Meet me at the van."

He was right. The number of photos was staggering. How did they ever solve a crime looking at all of these? She was most interested in the ones of the crypt door before the world and his uncle arrived. She scrutinised them carefully. The door stood open about 4 or 5 inches. She peered at the ground.

"Could we make these bigger?"

A couple of taps and the image zoomed in.

"Move it around a bit."

The ever-obliging Bruce did what he was told. Shona moved in closer to the screen.

"Stop."

The image froze.

"Bingo. Footprints. Could you screen shot that and send it to me? Send all the photos as well."

"They're probably our gravedigger's footprints."

"They look like they're different sizes. So unless our Mr Lassiter brought a companion with him we might just have our perpetrators footprints."

153

The limitations of space meant one person only in the tomb. This left the rest of them swinging in the wind. Shona set them on a search of the area. Once again they split into teams and took one quadrant each. Shona and Abigail had the one furthest away from the body.

"Ma'am, if Mr Gravedigger cleaned the place up, are we not wasting our time?"

"Probably, but it's our job to search the place corner to moss covered corner."

"I'm not one to moan but I'm boiling in here."

"Me too. I've sent for bottled water."

"According to Alexa the heatwave will break soon."

"Good old Alexa, I'll treat her to a drink."

"You'd be hard pushed. She's a computer."

"You say I'm weird? At least I don't talk to computers."

The witty banter accompanied eyes and heads down, searching the ground, the gravestones, the graves themselves and anywhere their murderer could contaminate. Or any member of the public supposed Shona.

"This is like searching for a needle in a barn full of haystacks."

"You'd noticed."

Anything they did find was bagged, tagged, logged into evidence and placed carefully in boxes in the back of the van. Angus had agreed to take all the evidence through to Dundee for them. For this, Shona was eternally grateful. It was too hot to be running around the countryside swapping and changing vehicles. The body would be taken to the mortuary in Dundee, where it would await Mary's tender ministrations.

Body number four is going to ramp this up way more than is comfortable. She could see a conversation with the chief in her future. One where she begged for more personnel.

42

They returned to the station via Visocchi's Ice Cream Parlour in Broughty Ferry. Completely out of their direction home, Shona didn't care. Desperate times called for desperate measures. They jumped the long queue by flashing ID cards. Sometimes being in the police had benefits. She chose double chocolate chip, vanilla and caramel. Abigail chose three scoops of strawberry. The woman behind the counter gave them an extra scoop each. They sat by the sea and ate them with relish. The sea was a smooth expanse of blue glass. Tayport, on the other side of the river, looked idyllic bathed in the sun's rays. Life didn't get better than this.

"There's nothing like an ice cream to boost the spirits. This is even better than the stuff we ate in Skye. I didn't think this was possible."

"Couldn't agree more. Best ice cream in the city."

Despite the time out they ate quickly. Time, tide, or murder investigations waited for no woman.

Bruce was as good as his word. The photos got to the station quicker than Shona. She downloaded them on to the system and they were soon looking at them in glorious technicolour. In the redecoration the force had splashed out on a 5K screen. Every shot could be viewed in perfect pin sharp detail.

"I guess Lesley King isn't missing any more," said Nina.

"Doesn't look like it," Shona responded. "Although we'll need DNA to confirm."

"I'll get a warrant to enter her flat and take her

156

hairbrush into evidence," said Iain.

"Great stuff, but someone else will need to do it. I've something else for you."

She tapped the mouse and a new photo appeared. "Analyse these for me. Get all the details you can. See if one or both of them matches the gravedigger."

He rubbed his hands together. "Something to get my teeth into."

Nina helped her prepare a feast fit for a king. This involved a pot of Earl Grey tea and assorted cakes she'd brought back from the Ferry, as Broughty Ferry was fondly known.

"Do you think it will work?"

"If the Chief Constable's still here, yes. If he's skedaddled, not a hope in hell's chance."

"What's your preferred outcome to use the corporate crap they come out with?"

"More warm bodies on the ground, guards for all the cemeteries and a villa in Florida."

Nina's laugh could probably be heard throughout the station. "Can I come and visit you in Florida as that's the most likely outcome?"

"You're not helping."

"You want me to do what? What universe are you living in?"

"I can't get moving on this case without more manpower."

"Shall I knit them? Conjure them out of mid air? Draw them? You tell me."

Shona thought it was wisest to say nothing.

"Believe me when I say, that pales into insignificance when measured up against your other hair brained scheme. Private security guards?"

"We're more likely to catch our killer if we cover

all the cemeteries, Sir."

"Do you know how many cemeteries there are in Dundee and Angus? Then we'd have to cover Perthshire and Fife as well. It must be hundreds."

"It's worth it to stop more murders."

"Would you like to explain to the Chief Constable why the bills for this station have rocketed into the stratosphere?"

"I still say it's worth it to keep people alive. You can't put a price on someone's life, Sir."

"Consider the ethical and moral argument of the greatest good for the greatest number. Keeping my department solvent will ensure that."

"This is people's lives we're talking about here. They're not numbers. We have a duty to protect them."

"McKenzie, I need to look at the bigger picture. If you want to guard the cemeteries do it yourself. Now, get out of my office or you'll be kicked off the force."

I'd like to kick him right in the unmentionables and into an unmarked grave. How the hell does he expect me to solve a flaming case without the necessary manpower? Stupid sod needs to shove his bigger picture right where the sun don't shine.

43

Shona slammed into the office and stormed over to Roy's desk. "Give me something. Anything."

"On what, Ma'am? I've arranged for uniform to pick up Lesley King's hairbrush. I've not had time to do anything else."

"You can work out how we can secure a couple of hundred cemeteries with a seven man team for starters?"

"Er..."

"You're right. Can't be done, can it? Look into every nook and crannie of our victims' lives. I want to know if they even sneezed."

She stomped over to Nina's desk. "Get those friends of Cara's back in here."

"Ma'am—"

"Now."

Nina threw a puzzled look at Abigail, who shook her head.

"Of course, Ma'am."

"The others had their heads down. "Abigail. I want every single neighbour within a mile radius of Lesley King's home, interviewed."

Without waiting for a reply she continued. "Jason, I want you, and Brain Gevers if I can borrow him, to speak to any person in the vicinity of Forfar Old Churchyard."

They all sat stock-still and stared at her.

"Move."

They all leapt to their feet and scurried off.

"What can I do, Shona?" Peter said, his voice gentle.

"You can think of how we can move this blasted case forward. You can also ask Mrs Smith and her daughter to come back in. It might be worth chatting to them again."

By the time she got to her office she was shaking so much she spilled her coffee.

"That's all I flaming well need."

She cleaned up and phoned her counterpart in Glasgow. She was on hold listening to *I shot the sheriff* on loop for several minutes before they managed to find him. By this point she could have shot every bally person in this case, never mind the sheriff and his deputies.

"Shona McKenzie here, from Dundee. I believe my sergeant spoke to you?"

"He did that, Shona. I've known Peter for years. Good chap."

"He certainly is." She forced herself to stay calm and play nicely. This poor bloke wasn't the cause of her woes.

"Did you manage to speak to Sal McLintosh?"

"That's going above and beyond, Shona. McLintosh makes Attila the Hun look like a teddy bear. She's a complete nutjob."

"So you haven't spoken to her?"

"I didn't say that. We did bring her in for a wee chat."

"And?" She shuffled in her chair and looked at he clock on the wall. *Could he draw this out any more?*

"And I think I'll be in debt to her and her mental family for the rest of my life."

"Did she have anything to say about Barry Grisham?"

"She helped Barry out with a loan. Turns out he's not so keen on paying it back. I'd say his life expectancy may not be in his favour."

"Does she know anything about his girlfriend?"

"Says not, but I suspect she's lying through her teeth."

"Do you think she had anything to do with Cara's death?"

"Not her style. If she'd taken a hit out on Cara the lass would have died after an altercation with the business end of a gun."

"Thanks. You've given me something to think about."

She thought about asking Sal McLintosh to take out a hit on the chief.

44

Four Weeks Previously

Twisting her long blonde hair between her fingers the young woman stepped outside the door. She was alone but despite the dark night, not afraid. What a night. If her granddad knew she was here he would kill her. She'd be grounded for the rest of the year. She didn't care. Her eyes sparkled at she thought of the night she'd had. The swirling, writhing bodies packed the dance floor like the demons her granddad was always warning her about.

She walked slowly up the deserted road. Streetlamps lit her way. She knew she should keep to the main streets but youth made her brave. Or foolish. She turned into a dark alley and her steps quickened. Her heart thumped. Why had she come this way? Her pace speeded up. What was that? A crisp packet rustling under the weight of her high heels. A cat ran in front of her. Startled she cried out. Shadows danced against the wall, at one moment growing larger, the next fading. More demons. They were following her this night. She pulled her thin jacket closer and hurried as fast as six inch heels would allow. Her granddad would kill her for buying these shoes as well. She was so dead.

After what seemed like hours but was a mere few seconds she broke out of the darkness and into the light once more. Her heartbeat steadied and her pace slowed. As she tottered on the high heels her thoughts turned once again to dancing and to the alcohol she'd consumed. This was her first real night out and she couldn't be happier. She thought of the men she'd danced with, and the women too. This was open, free, no rules. Not like at home. That was all rules to follow and chores to be done. Home was horrible with a granddad who didn't care. Not like her new friends. They loved her. They wanted her to be happy. A song broke free from her lips. From the top ten, she knew every word. A beautiful voice which showed her training, but slurred from too much vodka.

She turned and walked across a near deserted car park. Two solitary cars lay abandoned, their tyres long gone. The owners were past caring. Stickers 'Police Aware' had been there for weeks. "I love my life," she called out into the sultry night. No one was near enough to hear her.

Or so she thought. A dark figure watched from the shadows. Not just watching but following her. He had been doing so for some weeks. It was he who suggested she broke her bonds and spread her wings that night. Break away from the controlling influence of those in authority. Yet they had never met. The anonymity of the Internet meant you could be whoever you wanted to be. Metamorphose into a young girl facing similar problems. Urge each other on to break the rules to break out of the chrysalis. Then, at the last minute tell a sorry tale.

"I've been caught. That doesn't mean you can't go. Live life tonight for both of us."

The foolish girl readily agreed.

So there they were playing a dance of death. She did not yet know she was part of a dance, but she soon would. He waited until she took a shortcut through the dark park. This was the quickest way home avoiding the long tangle of streets. She struggled to walk in the heels. Paths covered in chuckie stones were meant for sensible shoes. One heel got stuck. She pulled it out. A few more paces and it stuck again. She twisted trying to release it.

He stepped from the shadows. "I will help you."
    "No. No. Leave me... Oh it's you. Thank you."
    "Let me walk you home. You must lead the way."

There was only one demon that mattered that night. She had just met it.

45

By the time the team returned, Shona had calmed down. She wasn't quite back to her affable self but close. The station was teeming with people for her to interview. The cacophony lured the chief from his lair.

"What on earth is going on? Why does my station look like a train station at rush hour?"

"The lack of personnel means we have to interview all the witnesses here. They are waiting for their interviews."

"Did it not occur to you to stagger them?"

"Not at all, Sir." the gleam in her eyes said otherwise. McKenzie 1. Chief 0.

The Smith's had appeared as requested. Given that every single member of her team was currently occupied, she borrowed Brain Gevers to join her in the interview."

"Shona, you've got to stop using my coppers like you own them."

"Don't exaggerate. Its just Brian I use like he's my own."

"Did Debbie seem all right to you lately?"

"She was in a great mood. Said she'd just booked a holiday to Australia," said her mother, who then fell silent.

"Did she indicate who she was going with?"

"No. She never told us much about anything she did." The sister's voice held more than a hint of jealousy.

"Do you know anyone who could have held a

grudge against her?" enquired Shona.

"No. Everyone loved her. She was the life and soul of the party. Had a lot of friends. I can't see anyone wanting to hurt her."

"Did she ever mention any of the clients she met at Cat's Eyes?"

Mrs Smith stared at the floor and mumbled. "No. She kept that part of her life to herself."

Shona knew there was something the sister was dying to divulge.

"Mrs Smith. Do you mind if I speak to Lydia alone?"

The woman threw her a look filled with suspicion.

" I don't want to distress you any further. I'll get someone to take you for a coffee."

"I'm a tea drinker." She stood up.

"PC Gevers, find someone to look after Mrs Smith."

Shona waited until Brian returned before continuing with the interview.

"Lydia, it's important I know everything about your sister."

"She broke mum's heart. We're a God fearing family."

"It must have been tough for you both."

"In lots of ways. All that money she made and she never gave a penny to mum. Just like our wastrel father."

"Is your father still alive?"

"Drank himself to death. She was heading that way as well. I'm surprised liver failure didn't kill her."

Did she have a boyfriend?"

"She said not, but I knew different."

"How so?"

"I saw her several times."

Sounds a bit like she was stalking her sister. "Can you describe him?"

"About four, maybe five, inches shorter than her. Blonde hair. A bit stooped." She stopped abruptly.

"Anything else?"

"No." Her eyes screwed up, she thought for a minute. "Actually he was a bit over the hill."

"Did she ever let a name slip?"

"Nope, completely buttoned up."

"Your mother said that Debbie was happy. Would you say so?"

"As a pig in muck. She could splash the cash whenever she wanted to and one item of her clothing cost more than my monthly wage."

The green eyed God making an appearance.

"The good things in life were important to her. That song 'Where do you go to my Lovely' could have been written about her."

"Thank you, Lydia."

She left the witnesses to stew. This might make them more forthcoming when they finally got into an interview room. She made sure they all had plenty of water, before calling her team into the briefing room.

"What's the state of play?"

Before she got any further there was a knock at the door. It was the chief's secretary.

"Duty Sergeant's trying to get hold of you. Asked if you could go downstairs?"

"Does it have to be right now."

"I'm the messenger. If you go down it'll be over in a jiffy."

She held the door open and looked back. "You lot, get all this down on the boards and be ready to give me a briefing. I won't be long."

"There's someone you need to speak to." He pointed to a man sitting in the corner.

Shona took in his appearance, grey hair and wearing a suit. He looked defeated.

"Has he got info that will help us solve the case?"

"Possibly."

"Could you be any more enigmatic?" She stared at the sergeant, whose instincts she trusted. He stared back, unblinking. Many years of staring down the jetsam and flotsam that washed up here meant he was an expert at this game.

She broke first. "Okay."

"His name's Mr Stephens."

She introduced herself and asked the man to come with her. He followed without a murmur; steps slow and with a slight limp.

With a sigh he slumped down on the hard chair she offered him.

Worn out oxfords with a shine you could use to apply your lipstick.

"Military man?"

"Ex Black Watch. How did you know?"

Her gaze moved to his shoes. "Old habits die hard."

A wistful smile and a faraway look in his eyes. A trickle of saliva escaped his twisted mouth. He wiped it away with a trembling hand.

"I'd rather face the enemy any day, than raise a teenager." His word's were hesitant as though he was searching for them.

"I hear you. What can I do for you, Sir?"

"My granddaughter's missing."

Why did the duty sergeant feel this was her baby? They'd usually been found by the time she got involved, and not in a way with which any relative was happy.

"How long has she been missing?"

"Four weeks."

"How old is she?"

"Seventeen."

"Why haven't you reported it until now?"

"I've been here every day. No one knows anything. They think she might have run off with her boyfriend."

"You don't?"

"I didn't even know she had a boyfriend."

"What is your granddaughter's name?"

"Stacey Fellows."

"Will you excuse me for a moment?"

She grabbed a passing copper and asked him to arrange a drink for the old man, then slipped into her office. She logged into the missing persons database and was soon looking at Stacey's file. The picture gave her the answer as to why the girl might be part of her case. Long blonde hair framed a face so stunning she would give Aphrodite a run for her money. Bingo. Their killer with a fetish might just have struck again.

The young girl's grandfather looked like the very heart of him had departed. A tear rolled down his cheek. "I tried to do my best for her."

Shona's heart contracted.

"Tell me about her?"

It turned out Stacey's parents had died in a car crash two years ago. He became her guardian. She was strong willed and wanted to be out with her friends all the time. He was terrified something would happen to her so kept her close. She'd snuck out about four weeks ago and hadn't been seen since.

"Do you think she's run away?"

"If she did she's left all her clothes and the teddy

she's had since she was born. Since my daughter and son in law died, she's slept with it every night."

Shona had to agree it sounded more like foul play but she didn't articulate the thought. She might as well leave him with some vestige of hope.

"Mr Stephens, I can assure you we will do everything we can to find your granddaughter."

Even Shona thought it sounded like a platitude.

46

The team took her orders to heart and the boards were bursting with information. They'd started to draw lines between any similarities. So far, most of the dead were blonde. Some had been raped post mortem. Nothing else seemed to link them. Or did it? A couple had connections to the Alexyeyevs, but that wasn't unusual in her investigations. They seemed to come out of the woodwork whenever she put one foot in front of the other. She wondered if Pa Broon had a relationship with any of them, apart from Tommy and his lodgings. Probably. The man was like a bad smell only twice as difficult to get rid of, and more toxic by a thousandfold.

"When we interview loved ones, friends and neighbours, find out if there's any connection. Did they go to the same church, clubs, schools, or organisations, anything at all? There has to be something"

They drew up a list of general interview questions; otherwise they were free to use their judgement.

"Split into pairs. Use every legal trick you can to get the maximum information from them."

They all stood up.

"I'm not finished. Sit down."

After they'd obeyed she continued. "Roy, what did you come up with on your search on our victims?"

Roy tapped on his iPad a few times.

"I'll take them one at a time. Debbie Smith."

Shona nodded.

Abigail stood up, picked up a white board pen and paused at the relevant part of the board.

"I've looked into Debbie's social media accounts."

"Looked or hacked," said Jason.

"I had a warrant, big mouth."

"Boys, this is no time for bickering. Stop it this instance. I've about one nerve left and you pair are twanging it more than I need or want." *When will this infernal arguing ever stop. I should have got a job in a nursery. It would have been a hundred times easier and with better hours.*

"As I was saying, Debbie Smith's social media accounts." he tapped on the screen. "Seems she thought she was better than the rest of her family. Wanted the high life and would do anything to get it."

"Including working at Cat's Eyes?" said Nina.

"Including prostitution. High class, but she was still a prossie."

"And she put this on social media?" Shona's voice contained more than a soupcon of surprise.

"Private messaging. Some of her 'friends' on these platforms are not people you'd want to meet down the docks. They'd slit your throat and then steal your gold fillings."

Nina said, "I'll take her. See what I can shake out of her relatives and friends. Jason, you can join me."

Roy continued. "Next up. Cara Ballieri."

"Spill," said Shona.

"Again, Social Media—"

"You're like some sort of voyeur."

"Jason, that's enough. One more snarky comment and you're off the case. Are we clear?"

"It was a joke. Sorry."

"No one's laughing. Carry on Roy."

"No great detail or specifics, but I'd say she was playing an away game as well as a home game. Let's just say our Barry wasn't the only love of her life."

"Have you got a name?"

"As I said, no specifics."

"Roy, you and I will take Cara. I'm in the mood for a tussle with Barry. I think he's our man for that one. Let's see if he's got any links to the others."

"Tommy McShane. He is on social media but intermittently. Looks like he's using a mates computer or the ones at the library."

"Librarians usually know a fair bit about people. Especially round here," said Nina.

"Good spot. Although I didn't think you knew what a library was," said Shona.

Nina drew herself up to her full height and said, "I'll have you know I was registered at a library when I was one day old."

"That disnae mean you know how to use them."

"Everyone's a critic."

"Enough of Nina's reading habits. Tommy's life?"

"They were living hand to mouth. Had to use the Foodbank a couple of times, and resorted to food from skips on more than one occasion."

"What a way to live."

"Loved his brother though and would do anything for him, Hence him turning tricks."

"Find out if wee Charlie's back from the summer camp. Get him and Blaze in for a chat."

"Finally, Lesley King. Not a dicky bird on social media or the Internet about her, apart from one mention. She won Council employee of the year and *The Courier* covered it."

"Jolly nice of them."

"I keep telling you, Ma'am. They're no' that bad."

Shona ignored him. Why let the facts get in the way of her hatred of the press.

"I've tried every which way and still nothing."

"Looks like we'll have to resort to the human touch on that one. Peter and Abigail, she's all yours. Oh, and could you check out the video footage of Roy's wee accident at the lap dancing club?"

"We could leave it for a while. Keep them under lock and key."

"Much as I love that idea, Margaret McLuskey would have me handing in my ID quicker than you could say mistreatment."

47

Barry looked like he'd been scraped off a scaffie's shoe.

"Had a battle with the sauce, and it won then?" said Shona in a voice a trifle louder than necessary.

"It's not alcohol, it's grief."

"You smell like a pub after the punters have been kicked in to touch."

"Great description, Roy."

"Could you please get to the point? I'm not a well man, yet I am still willing to assist the police."

"Another word."

"I would like my lawyer. I'm sure you'll appreciate why."

The oily and smarminess were back. This bloke was well and truly getting right up Shona's bonnie Roman nose.

"Already sorted. Angus should be here any minute."

With perfect timing there was a knock at the door and in strode Angus Runcie. He was wearing a new suit in light blue pin stripe. It was dazzling under the florescent lights.

"Looking natty, Angus." The thought of a tussle with Runcie and his low life client had cheered her right up.

Runcie sat down. "We are not here to discuss my choice of my apparel. Why is my client here again?"

"To ask him some more questions about his relationship with Cara Ballieri." She lifted up a file, which she waved in front of the accused and then slammed on the table. "And I've a strong suspicion your client is up to his stethoscope in something dodgy and I intend finding out what." The cheery tone had hopped out the door and stainless steel had moved in.

"You can't say that. You have no proof."

"I just said it. Now, if you'd keep that mouth of yours closed we might get to the bottom of why I asked him to come in."

Tired of pussyfooting around she went straight for the jugular.

"What's this I hear about your girlfriend playing around?"

"Rubbish. Utter tosh." His oily smile appeared. "I'm sure we can sort this misunderstanding out."

"I don't think it's a misunderstanding." She opened the file, took out a sheaf of papers, and studied them. "Yep, definitely got two on the go."

"You're lying. There's nothing on that paper." The smarminess was beginning to slip.

She laid them face up on the table. "Plenty of writing."

He made a grab for the documents and she deftly slid them away. "I'm afraid not, Barry. These are your girlfriend's private papers. No peeking."

Barry lunged over the table and gripped the edge of the papers. Shona held tight and the sheet ripped in two.

"Now look what you've done Barry. Destroying evidence. Tsk. Tsk."

Roy yanked the man back. "Sit down. One more move towards the Inspector and I won't be able to restrain myself."

Barry thudded back into his chair, and then leaned forward his arms on the table. Clenched fists showed white knuckles.

"That's some temper you've got, Barry. That's

evidence you've just destroyed. That's called suppressing and tampering with evidence."

"It was an accident."

"Didn't look like that to me." She turned to Roy. "Did it look like an accident to you?"

Roy shook his head. "Looked deliberate."

Angus Runcie leaned forward and looked her straight in the eye. "I know you like to play fast and loose with the law, Inspector, but you are baiting my client. I insist you stop."

Far be it for her to agree with Runcie but he had a point. *I really will be out on my ear if there's another complaint about me. Shame really as not only does this sort of interviewing get results, it's also great fun.* She switched tack.

"So, Mr Jones. Can we discuss your change of name?"

Shona had never seen the colour drain from anyone's face so quickly before. He didn't utter a word.

His lawyer stepped in.

"What are you talking about? More fabricated stories with which to annoy my client."

"He hasn't told you, has he? You might want to have a chat with boyo here before we go any further."

Runcie looked like he'd been thrown in a cowpat. He always looked like that but the look was more pronounced, and mixed with that of sour lemon sucking.

"You are the most ill bred person it has ever been my misfortune to meet."

"I take it you don't like me much? I'm sure I'll get over it."

Runcie whispered in his client's ear."

"Now, now boys. You know everything said in here has to be out loud. We've a video recording that wants to keep your immortal words for the record."

The lawyer straightened up, looked down his nose at her, and said, "My client and I would like some time alone."

Shona shuffled her papers, and picked them up. "We'll give you twenty minutes."

On the way out of the door she gave them a cheery wave.

"Ma'am, I don't know how you get away with it."

"Sometimes, Roy, neither do I. Might have something to do with the fact I've licked you lot into shape." She smiled and Roy grinned back.

"Also my clear up rates are stupendous."

"Your crime rates on the other hand…"

"Touche."

48

This gave Shona time to visit the ladies room and grab another coffee. She sent in hot drinks to Runcie and Barry as well. Might stop him reporting her to the boss. She might think it was fine sport to bait Barry. The chief was likely to take a rather different view. There was a note on her desk from Peter, stating the CCTV files were in hand. Despite McLuskey's assurances of access the twins had refused. The sheriff stepped in with a warrant. They'd be there within the hour.

"There is a God and he loves me."

The thought of thugs 1 and 2 cooling their jets for a while longer was the best news she'd had since this case, or cases, started.

Runcie looked like he'd swallowed a wasp. "My client will cooperate fully."

"Jolly magnanimous of him. So, Mr Jones, your name change?"

"I changed it legally. It's Mr Grisham."

"Ah, now there's the thing, Barry. When you chose the name Grisham you chose to pass yourself off as a long lost relative of the writer. Him being a lawyer and all, I'm sure he'd take a dim view."

Barry looked like a bunny in a trap.

"Don't worry. We're not going to be telling him."

She gave him a few minutes to absorb this vital piece of information. His colour returned to normal. *I'd agree you're not a well man, and I'd bet my pension it's not just down to alcohol. What are you up to sunshine?*

He'd barely had time to recover before she asked, "Talk me through the reasons for your name change."

This time she thought he'd pass out. It might be worth handling a bit more gently.

"It was a very difficult time in my life. I don't want to relive it again. I am sure you will understand." Mr Smarmy was back.

All thoughts of gentle handling flew out of the window.

"It wasn't the best of times for your patients either. Being in a coma and being sexually assaulted by you wouldn't exactly be at the top of my things to do."

Barry opened his mouth. Before he had a chance to say anything, Runcie stepped in.

"My client did not sexually assault anyone. The allegations related to a couple of incidents which arose whilst bed bathing patients. This is a natural job for a nurse."

"Why the name change if he is so innocent?"

"I didn't want this following me around for the rest of my career."

"The fact you'd been accused of being a sexual pervert?"

"That's—"

"I think Cara got wise to you and you bumped her off."

She slammed a glass down on the table. Water splashed out. Even Roy jumped.

"You need to cough up someone who can vouch for your whereabouts the night of Cara's murder."

"I went home." He looked everywhere but at Shona.

She picked up the folder and waved it around again. "Choc full of evidence that says otherwise."

He stared at her, his eyes hard.

Shona had had enough. "Barry Grisham, I am arresting—"

"I was at Cat's Eyes."

"Why does that place keep coming up like a bad smell?" Barry just looked at her.

"Why didn't you say so before? I've a good mind to arrest you for wasting police time."

"My client—"

"I'm fed up listening to the pair of you. Get him out of my station."

As Barry got up she said, "Actually there *is* something else I wanted to ask you."

Half standing, Barry looked at his lawyer, who nodded. He sat down again.

She picked up another file from beside her. Opened it slowly and, equally slowly, pulled out its contents. Barry's eyes grew wider. She turned the photographs over and shoved one over the table.

"Do you know this person?" The photo was that of Debbie Smith.

"No."

"This one?" A photo of Debbie dressed as Raven.

"No." His eyes didn't flicker, indicating he was telling the truth. Surely if the lap dancing club was one of his haunts he'd know her. Maybe he was a better liar than they thought. Or, maybe he preferred blondes. In which case he could be a suspect for all the murders.

The answer was no to Tommy and Lesley as well.

"If I find out you are lying, there will be serious repercussions. Are we clear about that?"

"Crystal. I don't know any of them."

She stared at him until he started to shuffle. Picked up another file and looked inside.

Barry pulled at his collar, picked up the polystyrene cup and took a swig of lukewarm coffee.

She let him stew for a few seconds more.

Even Runcie looked anxious. "Have you got any more

business with my client?"

"I most certainly do. I hear your best pals with Sal McLintosh."

This time ghosts really did spring to mind. Barry gave a passing imitation of a stranded fish.

"What? How…?"

"Sal's at the top of our most wanted list. Not the sort of person you'd expect a nurse to be consorting with."

The stranded fish now looked like a beached whale. One that was about to gasp it's last.

"Are you okay, Barry?"

Silence, other than the man's laboured breathing.

"Mr Grisham."

Shona was about to dash for assistance when Barry spoke. "I'm fine. Just need a drink."

She was sure he meant a rum and coke, but poured him a glass of water and handed it over. He drank it like a Bedouin who'd found an oasis after weeks in the desert.

Runcie remained suspiciously quiet throughout all of this.

Once she was sure Barry was sufficiently recovered she asked, "What business did you have with our Sal?"

"Just that, business."

"Could you be more specific?

"She gave me some money to fund a project I am interested in starting."

"And this would be?"

"It is merely an idea at the moment. Embryonic."

"You're telling me that one of Scotland's most notorious gangsters gave you money for a project the founder doesn't even know anything about. Sounds like money laundering to me."

Her eyes narrowed. "Or illegal money lending

given the amount of debt you're in."

In a rapidly deflating balloon impression, Barry sank down into his chair. "I didn't kill Cara."

The jury was still out on that one, and all the other deaths. Shona changed tack again.

"I need you to provide your whereabouts for the following time frames." She reeled them off.

"How do I know? I can't remember that far back."

Then I suggest you come up with some way of remembering. Because if you don't I'll be digging even further into your life."

"You're threatening my client again."

"Are you half baked? What threat? I merely said I'd be looking into his actions as part of my on-going case."

Her gaze focussed on Barry again. "You really need to look at getting a new lawyer. In the meantime you can both work out where you were during the time frames in question."

She left them to it but sent in some more hot drinks. She didn't want death by dehydration on her conscience.

49

The remainder of the interviews still continuing, Shona found the squad room deserted. This left her to retrieve the digital footage that may prove Barry's innocence. A quick visit to the sheriff and, warrant in hand, she strolled to Cat's Eyes. The sun shone brightly and the good citizens of Dundee looked happy as they went about their business. The twins being safely incarcerated, she had the relevant footage on a memory stick in less time than it took to pull a pint.

Trawling through the footage was another matter all together. She'd settled down in the briefing room where she could print the image and pin it straight to the board. Ten minutes of watching scantily clad women writhing around a pole and she was ready to slit her throat. In lieu of that, she poured herself another Brazillian blend and rescued a cream cake from certain death in the fridge. She was sure it would rather end its life in the noble pursuit of soothing her soul.

Thirty minutes later and still no sighting of Barry. She ground her teeth. *This has to be the most boring job in the whole history of the world. How can these women degrade themselves like this? No amount of money is worth it.* The flats they lived in and the cars they drove would give her the answer. These girls liked the high life and didn't care what they did to get it.

Peter popped his head round the door rescuing her from death by boredom. "We're back and I think the others are almost winding up."

"Thank heavens. I need another stooge to take over. I'm not through the first recording yet and I've lost the will to live."

"Get one of the women to do it. They're more likely to keep their eyes on the customers."

"You're right, as always. It would take twice as long for the boys to do it." Half a beat then, "Especially Roy now he's foot loose and fancy free."

She'd spent enough time on Barry and his shenanigans. There were more little fishies to put under the microscope. Before they did, she had a brainwave.

"Why didn't I think of that before?"

"Think of what?"

"Let's get every cemetery in Dundee, Angus, Fife and Perthshire searched for signs of grave tampering."

"Do you not think that's a wee bitty over the top, Shona?"

"Okay, it just might be, so let's narrow it down."

"To where?"

"With your experience, what radius?"

Stroking his chin, Peter gave it some thought. "The furthest body so far was dumped in Forfar. That's roughly eighteen miles. I would give it a twenty mile radius, perhaps twenty five miles to be on the safe side.

She thought she'd better run it by the boss. For once he agreed with her. Probably because cost came out of the council's coffers and not hers. As always her was willing to play fast and loose with other people's money.

"This would be better handled higher up. I'll contact the councils for you. I'll make sure they know the urgency of the matter."

"Thank you, Sir. I appreciate it."

"It's part of the bigger picture."

For once, despite the bigger picture rearing it's ugly

head, she left his office without thoughts of hericide. The Chief was free to live another day.

This left her free to catch up on the interviews. They started with Lesley King.

"That poor woman didnae have much of a life by the sounds of it."

"Because…?"

"Her neighbours barely saw her. Colleagues say she kept herself to herself. Polite enough but didn't interact."

"Friends?"

"Not a sniff of one. Distant cousin loves in Shropshire. No other relatives that we know of."

"No one can live in complete isolation. Plus, I think she's done something dodgy with the cemetery keys. We need to ferret it out. Roy put something out on Facebook and Twitter asking for help."

He tapped his iPad and the screen lit up. "Consider it done."

"Peter, phone the cousin, or ask Shropshire Constabulary to interview her."

She tucked a stray strand of hair behind her ear. Up in a bun, even it had enough of the heat and was making an escape bid.

"Iain."

Lost in thought he was startled. "Sorry, Ma'am."

"Forensics back with the DNA from the hairbrush?"

"One and the same, Ma'am. It's a positive ID."

"Where were you?"

"Just thinking about something. I'm in the room now."

"Glad to hear it, anything you want to share with the rest of us?"

"Not at the moment, Ma'am."

"I'll trust you for now. However, if it's to do with this case, don't leave it too long. It could be important."

"Got it. Give me a couple of days."

50

Three Weeks Previously

Skinny, shaved head and jittery, he bounced up the hill. Not the type one would usually see so far from the city. The heat was severe, even at this late hour. He still wore a long jacket, pink and grubby. Sweat stains under his arm grew larger with every stumbling step.

"Gotta keep going. One, two. One, two. One, two. Gotta keep going."

Despite his exhortations to himself he stopped, swayed, wiped his face with the arm of the jacket. He gazed around as though surprised at his surroundings.

A sheep appeared at his feet, looking like a fluffy cushion in the moonlight. Chewed at his shoelaces. He kicked it away. "Stupid animal. Shoo."

The sheep trotted off. Halted. Looked back with accusing eyes and then resumed munching some juicy grass.

He commenced his journey and his chant. "One, two. One, two. Nearly there. One, two."

His hands shook as he batted flies away from his head. The flies that weren't there. He'd started life in luxury but life's circumstances brought him down. Brought him to this place and an appointment with fate.

The small bothy, bathed in silver from the moon, was a welcome sight.

"One, two. One, two. One two. One, two." He reached the front door. Ducked inside and looked around him. Scrabbling in a voluminous pocket he pulled out a package and placed it on the table. The usual instructions were to hide it in their secret place. Tonight was different. Tonight they would meet. His drug addled brain filled with as much pride as it could muster. This was his big chance. His chance to move up the chain of command. No longer at the bottom, but someone important.

He took his coat off and flung it on to one of the chairs. A bead of sweat trickled down his face and dropped to the floor. A splash of water and salt that stained the wood. Another followed. He used the edge of his t-shirt to wipe the moisture from his face. This done, he leaned back in the sofa and closed his eyes. And waited.

Outside, a lone individual pulled a packet of cigarettes from his pocket. Pulled one out, lit it, and inhaled deeply. It was time. He banged his head on the lintel stooping to get through the door. Scraped their head. Put their hand up and felt blood. Paid no heed. Inside it looked like the boy was asleep. Yet his eyelids opened at the first muffled sound. Obviously drugs had not dulled his hearing.

"Are you Scott?

"Yeh." He stood up and extended a hand. It trembled and he willed it to steady. His learned memory told him he should be polite. Especially to superiors.

The man showed it no heed. Holding out a gloved hand would seem strange, even to this uneducated fellow. This night was not meant for such clothing. Yet, the gloves were a necessity. Everyone knew about DNA. Did everything possible to prevent leaving it behind. Pulling out a handkerchief he dabbed at his face.

"Where is it?"

The young man pointed at the table. At the large brick of heroin, which lay white against the scarred dark wood.

He jittered and bounced, praying to he knew not whom, that he could have just a small amount for himself. Something to take the edge off.

Only a matter of moments later he was no longer begging for a fix. He was dead.

51

Before they had a chance to move on, the phone rang. It was the doctor from High Dependency at Ninewells Hospital. It would appear Pearl was responsive and in a fit state to be interviewed. Shona hightailed it up to the hospital and used her get out of jail free, police parking pass, to abandon the car at the entrance. Sometimes, being a police officer rocked. Other times, it made her want to throw a rock.

"HDU was some distance from the entrance, as were all the wards. The biggest teaching hospital in Europe meant a long walk whenever you visited. Unless, of course, all you wanted was reception and a bit of shopping. They were close by.

Pearl's doctor informed them that she was awake but still in pain. The medication meant she could be out of it at times.

"Is she going to be any good as a witness?"

"Coherent and lucid most of the time."

"It's the remainder of the time I'm worried about."

Pearl was in one of her coherent and lucid phases. There was some confusion as she thought they were there to ask about the beating she'd received.

"I was just walking up the road when..." She licked dry lips. "The Blackhill Gang jumped me." Her voice was a whisper.

"I'm sorry, what did you say?" Shona wasn't feeling quite so lucid herself.

"I was jumped." She paused. "Not as much as a word." Another pause. "Davy Blackhill."

Iain, stepped in. "Hi Pearl. We're not here to talk about

your recent beating. Uniform will come and do that."

Shona's brain caught up. "We need to ask you a few questions about something else."

The girl licked her lips again.

Shona called a nurse over. "Is she allowed a drink?"

The nurse held a straw to the girl's lips and she took a few sips. "What?" Her voice was marginally stronger but still rasped.

"Do you ever use the bothies round here?"

Even in the state she was in the girl managed to look incredulous. "Why… need
…ask..me ..now?"

"I know it seems strange. It could be important for one of our cases." She deliberately didn't elaborate. The woman had enough on her plate.

"Boyfriend takes me."

"When was the last time you were there?"

"Can't… remember."

"Last question. What's your boyfriend's name?"

"Scott McLuskey."

Iain and Shona stared at each other. *Where do we go with this?*

"When did you last see, Scott?"

"Few weeks."

"Is this usual?"

"Not so long."

She indicated she'd like another drink. Shona held the straw to her lips.

"Are you saying he doesn't usually disappear for so long?"

"Aye."

Did you not report him missing?"

But, the woman's eyes were closing. They'd get no more out of her for now.

"That's a turn up for the books," said Iain."

"Initially that's what I thought. On reflection it would explain why both sets of prints were there."

"I wouldn't have put them down as the type to go hill walking. In fact, unless Pearl's had a personality transplant that's the last thing she'd be doing."

"Not in the slightest. That's why we need to find out what Scott was doing in that bothy. I think it may be one of the reasons the Blackhill gang jumped Pearl. Who are they by the way?"

He explained they were a bunch of low lives whose entire reason for being was to terrorise women. Davy's the worst of the lot. He's only been out of prison six weeks."

They climbed into the car. When they were settled, Shona asked. "His crime?"

"Rape."

Give me strength.

By the time she returned to her desk the working day was long behind them. Everyone, apart from duty personnel, had knocked off. She took in the dark bags and lacklustre eyes of her team and sent them home as well. She informed Iain and Jason they should bring in Mark Insley and Johnny Parr on their way in to the station in the morning.

"I'd like them here by 8 a.m. The rest of you can come back then too. I still need a briefing on today's interviews."

The station was quiet as she left. It had emptied off the detritus of the city. Seemed like it would be filling up again before they even got going the next day. As she walked to the car she pulled out her mobile and rang

Douglas. Yes, he would provide food and whisky, was the answer. He would pick her up at her flat.

52

She awoke to the sound of someone hammering on her door. Her head beat in time to the banging of the fist. *Just how many whiskies did I throw down my neck last night last night?* She struggled out of bed and staggered to the door.

"Okay. Stop with the noise," she shouted through the door. The banging continued.

Roy stood on her doorstep.

"For heavens sake. What's with the racket?"

"We're on a shout and you didn't answer your phone. Your doorbell needs a battery as well."

Her neighbour's door opened. "Is everything all right, Shona?"

"Fine, Ron. Sorry about the noise."

"Just wanted to make sure you were okay." He looked Roy up and down. He obviously found him wanting as he stood and glared at him.

"He's gen up. A colleague. My phone battery died."

Ron left them to it and Shona dragged Roy inside. "What time is it?" She squinted at her watch.

"Five a.m."

"What's up? No wait. I'll have a shower. Make some coffee. Fill me in when I get back."

She hurried off and ten minutes later she was showered, dressed and looking more human.

"Spill." She took a mouthful of scalding coffee, swallowed and gasped. She added some cold water and took another gulp.

"Body found dumped in Barnhill cemetery."

"How does anyone find a body at this time of the morning? Aren't most people in bed?"

"You'd think so."

Roy's cheery voice worked just like nails on a chalkboard. She forced herself not to bite his head off. "Who was cosying up to a crypt in the middle of the night? I know there's a dearth of gravediggers but surely they weren't working in the dark?"

"A couple of young lads staggering home from a party."

"And they decided to take a short cut through the cemetery?"

"No, it's usually locked. They saw the door was open so egged each other on to go inside."

"And look for bodies in crypts? Are you having a laugh?"

"This one wasn't in a crypt. They tripped over it on top of a grave."

"At least we've not far to go. I can't believe the killer dumped a body almost on my doorstep."

"He's a brave laddie."

"Equal ops, Roy, could be a lassie."

Roy shuddered. He'd had to sit through three days of equality opportunity and diversity training. His punishment for not being politically correct enough. The most boring three days of his life, they haunted him to this day.

Two travel mugs of coffee accompanied them to their destination. Their breakfast consisted of a cereal bar each. Not quite the breakfast of kings but it gave them energy and shoved hunger pangs into touch. They drove in silence, Roy concentrating on the road, Shona nursing her hangover. She rustled around in her handbag and found some ibuprofen. She doubled the dose in an effort to stave off her headache. Her older brother, a doctor, got through medical school with this little trick. She should have run to the cemetery. It would be just as quick and would have kicked this hangover into touch. She resolved to swear off the demon drink.

The cemetery was lit up like a Christmas tree, despite the fact the sun was coming up. They'd obviously managed to rouse Eddie before her. He was awaiting her arrival.

"Shona, you need to get your work day sorted out. It's far too early for a body to be getting out of bed."

"I couldn't agree more. You might like to tell the villains that."

He patted her back and left her to get on with her task. The POLSA, in his usual efficient manner, had the area taped off and ready for the arrival of the Police Surgeon. As the victim was not buried in a crypt, but out in full view he had to be declared dead.

While she waited Shona enquired about the witnesses.

"In one of the flats across the road. Someone in uniform owns it and she opened it up for us." The POLSA pointed in the general direction of a new block of flats. "The pair of them are in a right state. There's no way we could have kept them here, Ma'am."

"Thanks Sgt Muir. I'll go and have a chat to them soon. Any observations from you?"

Looked like the chains around both gates had been lopped off with chain cutters."

"Chains?"

"Brand new, Ma'am. The council put them there as an added security measure."

"Our nutjob's not so much a nutjob as several steps ahead of us."

"He is."

"I think he or she works for the council."

"It's as good a theory as any, Ma'am."

Seamus Harrison appeared. Even at this early hour he was dressed in a tweed suit. He must have been dying of heat exhaustion. Yet he looked as fresh as the proverbial daisy. Shona, on the other hand, was doing a fair imitation of an ice cream at the end of its life cycle.

The police surgeon set to, and within five minutes had declared the victim dead.

"By the looks of his arms, I'd be telling you he's an addict."

"Accidental overdose?"

"Not unless he tidied up after himself. I had a look around. Not a needle or syringe to be seen. The pathologist will be able to help you there."

"Thanks Seamus, how are you enjoying Dundee?"

"It's a bit quiet to be honest. I was after thinking it would be busy if your boyfriend's to be believed."

"They've all been buried in Crypts. A blind first aider could tell they were dead. So, we've left you in peace."

"You be calling me anytime, now. Do you hear me? "

"Loud and clear."

"I need a bit of excitement in me life. County Cork's quiet when it comes to murder. I'd heard good things about the happenings here."

"Everyone has fifteen minutes of fame. I can't believe mine is associated with the highest murder rate on the planet."

"I'd be saying it's higher than Belfast during the troubles."

"Maybe I'll make it in to the Guinness Book of Records?"

His laugh could be heard in Broughty Ferry.

"Where is that fella of yours?"

"No clue. Obviously didn't fancy getting out of bed."

They stood looking at the body for a few minutes before Shona said, "Have you ever heard of bodies being dumped in a crypt before?"

"I can't say I have. We get our fair share of the weird and wonderful in County Cork but this is definitely a first."

"Would a body keep longer in a crypt."

"That would depend on how long it had been dead before it went in there, was the crypt dry or had water leaked in? All sorts of factors come in to play."

"Thanks, Seamus. I hope I don't see you again too soon. In a professional capacity of course."

"Probable cause of death for your bach lad there is broken neck. Unless the break happened post mortem."

"With this killer, it wouldn't surprise me. Post mortem seems to be where he gets most of his kicks."

Shona thought of another question. "Are you able to tell if he's been raped?"

"Not unless I disturb more evidence than you'd ever be wanting me to." He stroked his beard. He put a finger to his lips and patted his mouth.

"Come with me."

The pair moved back to the boy. Seamus looked at him and crouched down again. He indicated Shona do the same.

"Nothing official here mind."

"Got it, Seamus. You don't want to be quoted." Shona was now on her haunches taking in every word.

"Look at this." He indicated the boy's belt.

"Looks like they've been done in a hurry." The proverbial lightbulb went off in Shona's head. "Our killer was probably disturbed while finishing off."

"That's speculation my girl. You'll be wanting to get proper confirmation."

"I always did like the Irish, but I'm liking them more and more."

"Away with you. Have you kissed the Blarney Stone?"

53

Even without the evidence of the missing syringe, it was clear this young lad did not die of an accidental overdose. Not one administered by himself anyway. Skinny to the point of anorexia, he had been arranged on top of the grave. Shona's brain ran through all possible permutations of what could have happened to him. Did he overdose and someone was with him? Unlikely, another drug addict would have skedaddled, cleaning up and arranging the body, the last thing on their mind. . If it was their serial killer, why had he left the body out in the open air? These thoughts made her brain scream, *Seriously, I'm never drinking again.*

She crouched down and examined the body more closely. He looked about twenty five. Recently shaved his head, but it had time to grow into quarter inch stubble. She'd say it was done about a month ago, maybe longer given his state of health. Malnourished. Filthy dirty.

She stood up. "Iain, over here with the camera."

He trotted over and started clicking, happy as a puppy in a ball pit.

She watched him until a sultry voice interrupted her. At the sound a warm feeling swept over her body.

"Good of you to get here," she said without turning round.

Her shoulder was grabbed and she spun round. "Hello beautiful."

"That's Inspector Beautiful to you." Her eyes shone and her smile could melt ice.

"It seems your killer's not taken the time to inter this one."

"Looks that way."

Iain having finished with both camera flash and

clicking, they both bent down to take a look.

Shona gently picked up his arm, straightened it and pulled back the sleeve of his filthy pink jacket. . There were, indeed, track marks on his arm.

"Junkie. That might explain his general air of neglect."

"No defence marks to be seen. So, it doesn't look like he put up much of a fight," said Shona.

"Looking at the size of him I'd say he didn't have the energy to put up a fight of any description."

"You're right." Shona lightly pulled back his lips. Discoloured and rotting teeth, the mucosa pale, all added to the general air of neglect.

"I don't think dental records will help us identify this one."

"Not seen a dentist in years. I'm not sure why as he could have gone to the dental hospital."

"The poor lad probably had other things on his mind. Like where to find his next fix." Shona stared at him. "He looks vaguely familiar."

"Looks like he's got a broken neck. Second one so far."

Groaning, Douglas stood up and rubbed his back. "This sort of work is killing me. Might have to stay in my office."

"Big girls' blouse." Shona tried to ignore the fact her back felt much the same.

A search of the cemetery was ongoing, the others having taken the initiative. Shona examined the gravestone on the grave. She wondered if the deaths had anything to do with who was buried in them. *Now I'm clutching at several straws. Are we ever going to get a break?* The answer to this was work harder and think like a killer. That is what would give them their answer. Or sheer blind luck.

It was time to interview some witnesses. She grabbed Jason in the hope it would keep him out of mischief. It might also stop him getting injured. His innate ability to get injured would lead to him tripping over a gravestone and knocking himself out.

Her optimism was sadly misplaced. On the way up the stairs to the flat, he tripped over his own size nines and gave himself a fat lip.

"Jason, you are a serious liability. I can't believe the army let you loose with guns."

"I was one of their best shots, Ma'am."

"It's who you were shooting that bothers me. God help us in a war if you were the best the army could come up with."

When they entered the flat she took him to a window and had a look. "You'll live. Fill out an accident form."

"I've got one here. Never travel without them now."

"That's the most sensible thing I've ever heard you say."

The witnesses were worse than useless. A couple of seventeen year olds who thought they were hard lads. Returning from their first party, high on drink and bravado, they entered the cemetery for some fun. Literally tripping over a dead body had them shaking in the corner.

The PC who owned the flat, was concerned. "I think they need a medic."

"They need a strong coffee and a calm voice. You do the coffee, I'll do the calm."

He went off to oblige and she sat down beside the boys.

Her voice gentle she said. "I'm DI Shona McKenzie. You can call me Shona."

The boys' eyes widened and their pupils dilated.

"It's okay, you're not in trouble."

They stared at her not saying one word.

"Take some deep breaths for me. That's right. Well done."

The coffee appeared and they drank the sweet concoction without a murmur.

"May I ask you names?" Nothing taxing. Nothing to trouble them. Start with the simple questions.

"Paul Samson."

"Freddie Flintoff."

"Your not in bother so you can give us your real name."

The boy looked resigned. He pulled ID out of his pocket and handed it over. "My mother loves cricket."

Shona scrutinised it. That really was his name, poor lad.

On further questioning it turns out they'd seen someone else in the cemetery. A figure, not sure if it was a man or woman, dressed in dark clothes. They were in the distance hurrying towards the back of the cemetery.

"Approximate height?"

"About six foot."

"Build?"

What do you mean?" asked Freddie. His mate looked just as perplexed.

What do they teach them in school these days? "Were they fat, thin, anything else about them?"

"Solid. Like a boxer."

"Did you see or hear anything at all that might help us?"

The boys' eyes narrowed. Shona could almost hear the two few clogs in their heads grinding together.

A staccato tic appeared in the corner of Freddie's left eye. He stopped it with his middle finger, a reflexive action that told Shona this was a regular occurrence. "I could hear a police car, or something. Maybe ambulance."

This wasn't helping but Shona held her council. She gave time for the cogs to do a full revolution.

Paul spoke up, hesitant at first. "I think there was a funny smell." Then more confidently, "Yes, there was."

"Could you describe it?"

"Like smelly feet." He turned to his friend and shook his arm. "Remember. I said you needed to nick a bottle of shower gel if you couldn't afford to buy it."

Freddie's eyes lit up. "Aye. He did."

"Anything else?"

"No."

"No, nothing."

Said in unison.

"Thank you boys. The PC here will take your statement."

She looked over at the PC who nodded.

"Thanks for helping out."

She walked away wondering how they could catch a killer who evidently had an odour problem. That wouldn't be easy. Not.

54

Every move they made was being watched and analysed. Another flat had been appropriated. This time it was empty. A quick look through the letterbox showed a large pile of letters and junk mail. The owners were on holiday. A deft use of a card and the man was inside. The ability of the Scots to delude themselves with regards to the security of their property, made this job so much easier. This home provided him with the perfect hideout and the perfect viewpoint. A cold beer, straight from his hosts' fridge, sat by his side. Cold beads of moisture ran down the smooth sides. He wiped the bottle with a large handkerchief, which was then stuffed in a pocket. Took a long drink and swallowed. The sharp tang soothed and settled. Took the edge of the anger. An anger that was quickly pushed inside. Cold, calculated control was needed to do the job. Emotions only muddied the thoughts. Caused both mistakes and havoc.

Every movement, every heartbeat of the investigation crew was noted and recorded. Knowing how they worked, what made them tick, meant he could stay one step ahead. Could control the game and escape justice for his crimes. Get away with murder. In this case that was not a saying, but the truth. It was this ability to take control, to lead the way, was what helped him get through life. Helped in the formulation of a plan so beautiful it could not be faulted. Sitting there, in a small Dundee flat, the killer thought of this plan. So far it was faultless. Or was it? Maybe it was only luck that had favoured the idea so far. Maybe the next victim would be the one that allowed the police to join the dots. To finish the hunt and catch a depraved killer. Yet the thought of those still to come gave some measure of reassurance. Whatever happened there were several safe in their hiding place. Waiting for their chance to die. By now they were begging to die. To be released from their torment.

His thoughts turned to the two witnesses in the cemetery. They'd interrupted him. Stopped him completing his mission. This was unforgivable. Where was the pleasure in finishing quickly? Where was the pleasure in doing half a job? He was not in control and this bothered him. Made him anxious, which started the anger. His anger had now flamed into a white hot heat. There was only one thing that would relieve this. Death.

Little did they know that when they made a decision to enter through those gates, they entered into hell, where they met the devil himself. They had made an appointment with death.

The police seemed to be finishing up. The head one walked off down the path. Stopped beside a stunning black woman. They seemed to be talking.

Pocketing the glass bottle, the man walked out the door. Several streets away the green bottle was thrown into a glass-recycling bin. No one would find the correct DNA here. No one would look for it in the first place. It was too easy to keep these idiots in their place.

Treated like an imbecile, those with power said that his life would be wasted. Who were the imbeciles now? Only one person controlled this game with an intellect he was not given credit for. In the snap of a neck, that had changed.

His thoughts turned back to the two boys. He would have to search them out. Study their habits and work out what would entice them into his spider's web. This would not be difficult. Teenagers were now so easy to find and to befriend. They would not know that the friend they made online was the monster they met that night in a graveyard. A few cool remarks would be made. Butter them up. Give them compliments. Complain about how unfair life was. Slowly the web tightened.

Then one day they would be bound and tied in his hideaway. Ready for their game to commence.

55

Silhouetted in the clear blue sky the station looked almost beautiful. Shona thought that beautiful might be taking it a bit far but she was willing to give it the benefit of the doubt. She at least had some warm feelings towards it.

The warm and fuzzies continued even after a visit to the chief. He'd had a word with the council, hence the chains on the gate. All the bigwigs in Police Scotland were currently in negotiations to have all the cemeteries searched for extra bodies. She liked this bigger picture as it might give her a lead. One she hadn't thought of. Maybe the chief wasn't as bad as she thought.

The fuzzie feeling lasted long enough for her to get to the briefing room. Then reality crashed back in. They now had five murders and not a sniff of a suspect. Unless you counted Barry, who was still sitting on the sidelines. Humphrey Masterton turned out to be all mouth and no trousers. The Brothers Karamazov were paddling in the shallows but didn't seem to be in at the deep end. Then it struck her. The Alexeyevs were still locked up.

Peter took in her stricken face and said, "Is there a problem, Ma'am?"

By this point the others were staring at her as well.

"Did we ever examine the video footage of Jason's accident at Cat's Eyes?"

The blank stares gave her the answer. "On it now."

The next hour brought silence and their answer.

"Looks like soft lad tripped while they were

showing him the door," said Peter.

"They'd argue the bruises happened while they were helping him up," added Nina.

Jason had the last word. "The ba... baskets are going to get away with it."

"Peter, go and release them."

Thus was the way of the world when it came to Thugs 1 and 2, thought Shona.

Nina reported back that the rumours about Debbie being a high class call girl were true. She was funding her lifestyle through selling her body.

"Jist like Senga, but with more of the readies changing hands," said Peter.

"Obscene amounts of readies," replied Nina. "A thousand to two thousand a time it would seem."

Stunned silence took over until Abigail said, "Can I write my resignation letter now? I have a new calling."

"Is that per night?" said Roy.

"Per hour."

"In *Dundee*? I'm changing jobs as well. Who's got that amount of money round here?" Jason rubbed his hands together. "That's more than I make in a month."

"Never mind her income. Who was her pimp?" Shona brought them back to reality.

"I've not figured that out yet. I thought Roy might come up trumps with that one."

"Normally I'd go down the Duck and Dagger at the docks for that sort of enquiry," he said. "I don't think this one's going to be hanging out there."

"Check into the Alexeyevs," she ordered. "See if they're diversifying."

"Maybe she was her own pimp. Picked up clients at the club," said Iain.

Shona stood up and paced round the room. This case had her antsy. If she didn't release some energy she'd explode. "Good spot. See if the tapes show anyone she was particularly intimate with."

"Even I've had a gutful of those tapes," said Jason. He slumped down in his chair. "There's only so much you can take of women demeaning themselves."

Blimey, maybe the lad's growing up.

Peter fanned himself with *The Courier.* "We need to find more blowers for here."

"The thought of those women makes me come over all hot as well," said Roy.

The whole team burst out laughing, including Shona.

"Cheeky wee git. You know that's no' what I meant."

"Your wife would castrate you," said Nina.

"Aye. She would."

"Is Charlie McShane back from his travels yet?"

"Got back last night. Blaze is bringing him in later today."

"Good stuff. Abigail, you and I will interview him."

Thumbs up indicated her agreement.

Roy, see what you can find out on the Internet about the pimps round here." She paused for a beat, then, "Did we ever get a response on social media about Lesley King?"

"Okay to the first bit. Not checked yet to the second. I'll check it out now." He picked up his iPad and bounded out of the room.

"Nina and Jason, you're on tapes first off."

They both screwed up their faces as though there was suddenly a bad smell.

"Don't worry, we'll do it in spells."

"I'd like to put a spell on whoever's doing these murders." Nina stopped, then added. "And one on Cat's

Eyes for good measure."

"Wouldn't we all?"

She tapped her pen on the table then used it to point at Peter and Abigail. You're on missing persons. Let's see if we can figure out who this morning's corpse is."

"I feel sorry for the laddie. He might be a junkie, but he's still someone's bairn."

"It wouldn't surprise me to find out he's Mrs McLuskey's missing bairn, Scott."

56

Wee Charlie wasn't quite as thin as his brother but not far off. Shona hoped the Derbyshires had been feeding him. Blaze didn't seem the type to starve a child but you never knew. He was a bundle of twitches and tics. Not surprising considering everything he's been through in his short life. Shona considered the options for interviewing him. On the one hand was the interview room, which was cold and impersonal. On the other hand, said interview room contained all the recording equipment. She asked Blaze to wait for a few minutes.

"Abigail, find some toys, take them to the small room with the comfy chairs. Make it look a bit more friendly."

"I'll see what I can do, but I can't work miracles."

"Surely we must have something here in case there are any children hanging round?"

The sergeant managed to work wonders. She'd even found a wrapped present which, she informed Shona, contained a remote control truck. The wee lad could keep it.

"Sorry?"

"Uniform is collecting for the Foodbank. Some of them brought in toys. I nicked one."

"Your career as a criminal mastermind is off to a flying start. Any chance you could nick something else as well?"

"There were some books and a box of Haribo."

"You have my permission to relocate them to our department."

The room was, if not exactly cheerful, less threatening than it was. They piled the presents up in one corner. It was Christmas in summer, Police Scotland style. The interview was both long and heartbreaking. Charlie was a bundle of nerves and a stutter slowed everything down. He missed his brother and wanted him back. Why had he gone off and left him?

Yes, his brother had brought people back to the flat. What sort of people? He didn't know. He only knew they had nicer food the next day. Did any of them come more than once? Only the two men with the funny accents. They wanted money but Tommy didn't have any to give them.

Once the interview was finished, Blaze broke the news that Tommy was dead and wouldn't be coming back. Tears, bravely held back, started to flow down his cheeks.

They rolled down Shona's cheeks as well. Abigail and Blaze joined in.

Charlie stared mutely at the presents. When told he could open them he made an effort but his heart wasn't in it. He cheered up slightly at the sight of the truck and asked if he could take it home. The answer in the affirmative brought a hesitant smile.

He's just a normal wee boy. Maybe Blaze will help him to recover.

As though she had read Shona's mind, Blaze said, "We've started adoption proceedings."

Despite her strangeness, Shona thought the couple would be good for the wee boy. Someone to love him, a few square meals and a bit of stability would work wonders.

"Shona, that's possibly the most heart rending interview I've ever had the misfortune to sit in on."

Shona, trudging along the corridor beside her didn't have the emotional energy to respond. It was times like this that made her doubt her career choice. Stiffening her back she resolved to get justice for little Charlie. Whoever hurt this young lad's brother was a dead man, or woman, walking.

"You did well in there. It's tough when kids are involved."

"When I was in Skye we had a case where a three year old was snatched. She was found strangled two days later. Her parents threw themselves off a cliff the day after the funeral."

"How did you ever recover from that?"

"I don't think I fully have. Nothing could ever be as bad as that." A solitary tear rolled down her face. "We will catch this monster, won't we?"

"Yes we will." Shona's face hardened. "I can guarantee that."

She put a comforting arm around Abigail's shoulder.

57

Peter popped his head round Shona's office door, took one look at her, and disappeared. When he reappeared he was carrying a plate of assorted cakes and a large mug of coffee.

She smiled wanly and said, "You know me too well."

"Get a couple of those inside you."

He'd also brought himself a mug of the tar he called tea. He refused a cake and they sipped in silence.

Shona took a bite of a soft apple turnover. The flaky pastry melted in her mouth and mingled with the sharp tang of cooked apples. As she swallowed the last morsel she picked up a chocolate éclair. Bursting with cream it was the perfect antidote to her, so far, miserable day. She washed it down with a mouthful of coffee, the smell of which teased her senses and soothed her soul.

Once the seven million calories of fat and sugar had worked their magic, Shona said, "Have we got an identification on our lad from Barnhill?"

"Aye, we have. Or we have pending DNA and his mother's identification. It's Scott McLuskey."

Shona reached for a fruit slice.

Scott's mother was otherwise engaged. Tucked up in a rehab centre she couldn't be released to identify her son's body. That left Margaret McLuskey. Shona couldn't believe she would have to be nice to the woman. Then her innate compassion kicked in. The battleship might be the devil in disguise but she'd still lost a loved one. Even battleships must feel pain and loss.

Margaret agreed to come down to the mortuary and take a look a their latest body.

"I know this must be difficult for you. Thank you for coming." Shona held her hand out.

The compassionate words were wasted on the harridan, who totally ignored Shona and her proffered hand.

"Cut the crap. I'm only here because his worthless, sad sack of a mother has let him down. Again."

Shona felt like beating the crap out of Margaret, but bit her tongue. Slapping the bereaved was taken seriously in the force. Despite its ups and downs she rather liked her job.

Mary had the lad laid out as nicely as she could, given the circumstances.

Margaret stood for a moment and then said, her voice trembling, "Yes. That's Scott." She wiped a stray tear from her eye.

Shona put an arm around the woman's shoulders.

"I am so sorry for your loss, Margaret. Thank you for doing this for us."

The battleship reappeared and McLuskey shrugged her arm away. "His mother wasted his life. He'd have been better with us."

With that she stomped off, her bosoms billowing before her.

Shona stared at her retreating back, a frown on her face. Looks like there was trouble and strife in the McLuskey family. She intended finding out if it had anything to do with her case.

Mary asked if she could have a chat with her before she left.

"With pleasure. This is the coolest place in the city.

I'm just about ready to join the bodies in your drawers."

Although there was no air conditioning in her office, Mary left the door open and cold air from the mortuary seeped in. It provided a welcome chill to the otherwise stuffy air.

Mary, a woman who liked her creature comforts, had chucked soft throws over the furniture, making them a bright contrast to the stark inside of the mortuary.

Shona sank into a comfortable chair and sighed. "Can I move in with you until this heat dies down?"

"Be my guest. I'm sure Thomas wouldn't mind coming down here regularly to bollock you." Mary's eyes crinkled with laughter.

"I wish Thomas was here. For a short time before he was transported to his last resting place."

"Shona McKenzie I can't believe you just said that."

"Much as I'd like to sit in here discussing our Thomas's demise, you said you needed a chat."

"I didn't want to say this in front of the relative, even if it was Margaret McLuskey. Scott was raped post mortem."

"This is one sick killer we're dealing with. Seamus and I had a feeling that might be the case." She paused then said, "Did he have any scratches, bruises or cuts around about the top of his jeans?"

"It's not sick killer I'd be saying, but a stronger expletive." Mary moved over to her desk and woke her computer up. A few key taps and she said, "Yes. Consistent with rough handling."

"I've a feeling our killer was interrupted. The choice of body dump may have been more circumstance than planning."

" I can't say whether he was interrupted but I can tell you the jeans were probably pulled up rather more forcefully than I would expect if he did it himself."

"My other thought is that our killer is becoming more angry."

"Again I can't tell at first glance. However, I'll be able to get back to you later today with a more thorough report."

"Mary, you're a legend."

Mary flipped her head in dismissal. "There's one thing still puzzling me."

"What's that?"

"Lesley King wasn't raped, be it pre or post mortem. She was still intact."

"A virgin? In this day and age?" Shona's voice rang with incredulity.

"Definitely. Now, with that piece of information, I must get on. You seem to be keeping me particularly busy, but I've others awaiting my tender ministrations."

58

The remote location was perfect. The old house had numerous rooms, anterooms, dressing rooms and, most importantly, a cellar. This was the room where he thought up everything he would do. Its cold walls and dim interior inspired him. He had covered the walls with photos and diagrams. Photos of his possible victims. Diagrams of their movements. Lists of when he might snatch them. Ideas of how he could coerce them. Dates, times and places he might meet them. Which room he would keep them in until they met their demise and took up their rightful place in a cemetery. Which cemetery that would be, and why.

In pride of place were diagrams of all the cemeteries with detailed outlines of every grave. People taking notes in a cemetery were not unheard of. Many people research their ancestors graves. He had merely been one of them.

He sat at the table in the middle and surveyed everything around him. This soothed him and allowed him to think. Not all the rooms were full at the moment. He jotted down a few notes. Thought of some names and added them. Some possible places to find marks came into his head. These were jotted down.

He looked at the diagram of the rooms. Three rooms empty. One more would be disposed of tonight. That meant four he had to find, groom and rescue. Before he did this he had to plan his next body dump. Auchterhouse cemetery was top of his favourites list at the moment. Quiet and secluded, no one appeared to be around at night. All tucked up in bed asleep with not a

care in the world.
The place was decided.

He stood up and walked to the wall. Studied the chart of the current occupants. Now the only thing to decide was who would fill the spot he would prepare for them. It would be the perfect spot and they would take their place in history.

The embryo of an idea formed in his mind. It grew with frightening precision and then exploded into action. There was something he had to do. Something that would shock them all, and show them the extent of his brilliance. It would shift the balance of power without any shadow of doubt.

59

Nina and Jason were losing the will to live. They had nothing to report so far regarding a sighting of Barry. There were still several recordings to go. Abigail and Peter took over. Peter looked grim. This was not his favourite way to spend his working day. Shona had the urge to tell him to suck it up, but of course that was what he was doing.

They'd barely had time to settle to their task before the chief came to find her.

"Shona, I need a word."

This wasn't his usual bluster when she'd done something wrong, so Shona was somewhat puzzled.

They moved to his office, where he sat behind his mahogany desk and she stayed standing. This was her usual state when in his room. This made it easier to hoof it in a hurry.

"Please sit down."

She was beginning to worry. Had someone close to her died? Did he have bad news?

"The Chief's in the other jurisdictions have been getting back to me. It looks like we have two incidences where graves have been tampered with."

Shona couldn't move. This was getting worse by the minute. *How can we possibly deal with all of this as well as the cases we already have?*

"That's the bad news."

Shona managed to muster up a coherent sentence from somewhere.

"There's good news?" Not the best sentence in the world but the best she could manage given the circumstances.

"You need to keep this quiet." He waited for her response before continuing.

"Of course, Sir."

"There will be force wide reductions in personnel."

Shona managed a vocal range she didn't think she was capable of.

"I just can't see why that is good news."

"Because your team will not be included."

She let out a breath she did not know she was holding.

Her voice weak she said, "Thank you, Sir. I appreciate it."

"As you seem to be the busiest department in Scotland, the decision was made not to make changes to what seems to be a winning team." He stared straight into her eyes. "Even if some of your methods do seem to be a bit unorthodox."

For once, Shona thought it wiser to keep her mouth shut.

Thomas sat back in his chair and looked at her. It was as if he was considering something.

Shona waited it out. A murmer from her might just tip him in the direction of bollocking her. Best to go with the flow.

Eventually he said. "I know the news of the graveyards will put an extra burden on you and your team. I will request that uniform provide you with three extra constables to help you."

"Which cemeteries, Sir?" Her voice had regained its strength and she was once more in professional mode. "Also, can I choose the personnel?"

"Brechin Cemetery and Pitkerro Grove Cemetery."

"One of those is in Angus. Can't they investigate it?"

"No. There's been a sixty vehicle pile up on the Forfar Road. Angus are all hands on deck sorting that out."

"I can see that takes priority."

"With regard to uniform, they will work it out. You're lucky you're getting them at all. That will be all."

It would appear that they were back to normal. However, Shona decided to make one last plea.

"Please can I have Brian Gevers? He's worked with us several times and slips into the team without fuss or explanation."

"Don't push it, Shona. Now get out."

60

The chief had come up trumps and Brian Gevers reported to her office. He brought with him Kelly Chambers and Tessa Bone.

"These are my mates, Ma'am. I asked if they could come," said Brian.

"Nice to meet you both but we've no time for pleasantries. Brian, report to Sergeant Johnston. He'll split you into teams."

Shona found herself in the team heading to Brechin. Peter was driving, as he knew the back roads, avoiding the Forfar Road. It seemed that every other person in Scotland had the same idea.

"Are we ever going to get there?" Shona had the window open and was drumming her fingers on the sill.

"Ma'am, in these situations I try to remember, there may be fatalities in that incident. At least we're alive." Peter was his usual implacable self.

Shona felt dreadful. He was right; this was all a matter of perspective. In the big scheme of things, sitting in a car with the sun shining, wasn't the worst way to spend her time. In the back, Jason, Brian and Kelly were listening to music on their phones. Tessa had gone with the other team. *Brian and Kelly must think CID is a right doss.*

Somehow, Angus POLSA had managed to get a team, a gravedigger and some burly coppers to the site. They couldn't yet call it a crime scene, as no one was sure if a crime had been committed. They had wrapped crime scene tape around the area and posted another burly copper at the gate.

"What have you got for me?"

"Looks like that crypt's been interfered with." He pointed to a stone edifice which rose about three foot off the ground.

Shona peered at it. Then she got up closer and peered again. "How can you tell?"

"Sandy…" He gestured to an elderly man to come over. "…Will be able to tell you more. He was the one that found it."

Sandy, was aged about seventy, small, wiry and with a puckered scar running down his cheek.

He saw Shona staring at it. "Bar fight when I was a youngster. This sobered me up and got me going tae church. Best thing that ever happened to me, or I'd have been swinging at the end of a gibbet."

Shona shook her head. "Sorry, I'm not usually that rude." Then she laughed. "You're not that old. The last hanging in Dundee was 1889."

"Aye, and I'm no' exactly Jack the Ripper." He smiled and continued. "You'll want to know about that grave?"

She nodded and let him carry on.

He spouted forth about rock, moss, lids, and spaces until her eyes glazed over. She just about heard the last sentence.

"So, I'm telling you that lid's been lifted sometime in the last week."

"Have you touched it, or done anything to it?"

"No. The local bobby accompanied me. He watched my every move. I'd be inside a locked van by now if I'd touched a damn thing."

She thanked him and made a beeline for the POLSA. He was arguing with a group of mourners at the gate.

"What on earth is going on?"

"I need a word Ma'am." This was forced through

gritted teeth.

They moved about a hundred yards away.

"What's the problem?"

"That's the McKinleys, local tinkers and low lives."

"I take it there is one McKinley less today. Unless you count the one in the coffin."

"They're trying to bury their patriarch. Auld Ruairidh McKinley. Died of natural causes last week at the grand old age of a hundred and sixteen."

"Not keen on your interfering with that."

"Not in the slightest."

"Well, it's your crime scene. I'm happy to go with what you recommend."

"I think we should slip them fifty quid and send them to the pub. The undertaker will take Ruairidh back until we're ready for him."

"Kind chap then?"

"Not particularly but he's my wee brother. He'll do what he's told."

They scraped up the readies from the assembled company and threw in an extra twenty for good measure. Shona said she'd reclaim it and pay them all back. They all said they were happy to donate to keep the McKinleys out of their hair. Everyone but her seemed to know them. Once again she regretted not having been brought up in the town in which she was born. It left her local knowledge lacking.

A warrant to exhume the grave had appeared, but they were still missing a pathologist. Shona pulled out her phone and rang Mary. "Are you still covering Angus?"

"I always cover Angus, and I'm on my way. The traffic's foul. I think I've moved fifty feet in the last ten minutes."

"Drive safely, we're not going anywhere until you get here."

They grabbed bottled water from the car and handed it out to everyone. Uniform in particular slugged it down like dying men. When asked if they wanted more they nodded.

"Sergeant Isles, is there any chance of a photographer? Mine is in Pitkerro Grove in Dundee, doing much the same as us."

"He's on his way, Ma'am."

61

The photographer arrived first. She was the size of a ten-ton truck and weighted down with cameras of every shape and magnitude. Add to that the photographer's vest stuffed to the gunnels with more paraphernalia. *The woman must be close to heat exhaustion.* Yet, despite her florid face, she seemed otherwise cool, calm and collected. She had a quick word with the POLSA and commenced clicking.

Shona shuffled from one foot to the other whilst she waited for Mary. A van pulled up and out jumped more coppers. They pulled out a tent, erected it and started putting white crime scene suits inside. They still didn't know if this was a crime scene, but they were treating it as such until further notice. Shona wasn't used to doing so little. She retrieved another bottle of water from the car and drank it down. More to give herself something to do than any great desire to drink the place dry.

The cemetery was beautifully maintained with a mixture of old and new graves. Tall, leafy trees were scattered around the cemetery adding a beauty all of their own. Shona leaned on the magnificent gates and waited. The full glare of the sun beat down unmercifully so, she retreated to the shade of a tree. Her knowledge of all things horticultural was zero, so she had no clue what type it was. Whatever it was, she thanked God for it.

Peter joined her.
"The young uns are moaning fit tae bust. They're fed up waiting."
"Tell them to join the queue. All we're achieving

here is a suntan."

Peter had left his jacket in the car and was now rolling his sleeves up.

"*The Courier* says it's going to break soon."

"If *The Courier* says it, it must be right." *It'll be the only thing The Courier ever got right. Stupid rag. Although Adanna's not so bad.*

Just when Shona thought they should all pack up and go home, Mary arrived.

"I know, I know, I'm here now." She flew past Shona and Peter and in to the changing tent. She appeared 2 minutes later, having pulled the kit on over her shorts and t-shirt. Her stature gave her the look of a demented garden gnome.

"Lead me to the grave."

Shona pointed her in the direction and donned similar clothing. She followed.

By the time she arrived at the graveside four of the bobbies had a hold of the grave lid.

"On three. One… Two… Three."

They all heaved and the lid lifted easily.

"See, I told you it had been disturbed." Sandy's grin was out of place in such a sombre setting.

No one was paying any attention to him. They were all too busy looking at the contents of the grave.

62

Inside lay the body of a young woman, about thirty years old and wearing shorts and a t-shirt that said. 'Made in Prague'. She also had long blonde hair. Rake thin, apart from her stomach, which swelled under the t-shirt. To be more accurate, they were actually looking at the various body parts of a young woman. She had been chopped up and put together again like a jigsaw.

"Has our jigsaw killer been let out of jail?" asked Peter.

"Not to my knowledge."

Kelly's colour had changed dramatically. Chameleon like, her face mimicked the tint of the grass.

"Move. Now." Shona's voice left no room for argument.

The girl swayed.

"Brian, get her away from the crime scene. Find her some more water."

Brian grabbed the girl's arm and dragged her towards the front gate and the safety of the car.

"I want you both back here soonest," she shouted after them. "You're here to do a job."

She, Peter and Jason turned their attention back to the body parts. The torso lay in the middle with the head and all four limbs present and correct. Thinking of one of her previous cases she was thankful for this. She couldn't believe they were back to the butcher, if not the baker and the candlestick maker. *Why do all my investigations involve the weird, wonderful and downright depraved? Most DI's get nice cases that they can solve in a day. Done, dusted and neatly tied up with a bow that says 'closed'. No, I chose to come to Dundee where they specialise in doing things differently. Then* she felt sorry for her thoughts. Dundonians were actually a nice bunch who'd help you if they could and offer you their last plate of stovies. The thought of a steaming plate of mashed corned beef, potatoes and onion with a big dollop of HP sauce had her slavering. She forced herself to swallow. Her saliva dripping in the grave would not go down well.

The job was neat, as though done by someone who knew what he or she was doing. Shona leaned in closer, or as close as she could given Mary was currently doing the same thing. She was no expert but she was sure they all came from the same body originally. However, experience had taught her that it was best to keep an open mind on these things. Only DNA would tell the truth of the matter.

Mary had the area around the body secured and was directing the photographer. Every aspect of the body was quickly, but thoroughly examined and catalogued.

Kelly returned, holding her long hair up from her neck. "Sorry, Ma'am."

"First body?"

"Not quite, but the fact she'd been diced and sliced got to me."

Shona took in her improved look and asked Jason to do a search of the cemetery with her. "Stick to a radius of about four hundred yards."

She was of a mind that any evidence would be long gone, but it kept the pair out of mischief.

"Jason."

He half turned towards her.

"Keep away from the gravestones and any tiny pebble or plant you might fall over."

"I'm not that bad."

"You're a walking, talking liability."

Mary waved her hand to attract Shona's attention. With another imperious wave she beckoned her over.

"Your victim is now plural. She's about five months pregnant."

"I think we may be looking at the body of Nadia Badowski. Our missing council worker."

Mary bent back down and carried on with her task.

"I am going to get this bastard if it's the last thing I do" said Shona.

Mary looked up. She didn't even try to hide her shock. "That's the first time I've heard you swear."

"This case has me every shade of rattled you could muster. How can anyone be running around dumping bodies and not a soul sees them?"

"Shona, you know they must be leaving evidence of some description. I'm confident you'll ferret it out.."

"Maybe a ferret is what I need."

"Given the state of the body, I'm hoping this one wasn't raped post mortem."

The very thought of it made Shona gag. She left in a hurry. Everyone in the force has a breaking point. She had just found hers.

Peter seemed to be occupying himself talking to the gravedigger.

"Turns out he's a distant cousin of mine."

"I'm happy for you." Sarcasm dripped so strongly it could almost be classed as a stream. "Doesn't help much with the investigation though, does it?"

"You never know with these things, Ma'am. I've asked him to get the gossip from the gravedigger network. Someone might know something."

"Sorry. You're a top man, Peter Johnston. I don't know what I'd do without you to keep me on the straight and narrow. "

His baritone laugh performed percussion on the ancient gravestones. "Don't you forget it."

After spending a couple of hours searching in the hot sun, Brian and Kelly looked like lobsters that had slapped on oil to ramp up the tan. They carried several evidence bags.

"CID's not as exciting as you thought it would be? Less Gucci and more scutwork."

"At least in uniform you can take yourself inside and out of the sun occasionally. I don't know how you lot do it day in day out."

Shona didn't think they'd see Kelly volunteering for CID anytime soon.

"This is better than flooding. Then you'd really know all about it, lassie." Peter pointed to the evidence bags and said, "Take these to the car. We'll be there soon."

As she watched them walk off Shona said, "You're too nice to them. They need to harden up a bit."

Peter just smiled.

63

The return to the station was somewhat subdued. Kelly and Brian were thanked and, in Kelly's case at least, sped back to their normal duties. Shona rummaged through her bag and found some hand cream. She shut the door and liberally applied the lotion to every part of her anatomy that had been exposed to the sun. She wondered if she could sue Police Scotland if she got skin cancer?

The team at Pitkerro Grove took a lot longer to get back. Mary's delay meant they hung about for a lot longer. The choice of this graveyard did not fit the pattern. The graves were newer and there were no crypts to be found. In fact there was very little to be found, including trees and shade. Nina, showing some measure of initiative, took them all to Dobbies Café until POLSA phoned them.

On their return they had a similar tale to tell. The grave was next to the back wall. When opened up they found, under just a few inches of soil, the body of a young girl. Not just any girl.

"Looks like Mr Stephens' granddaughter isn't missing any more," said Nina.

"You think your body is Stacey Fellows?"

"I'd say so. I know, DNA and all that, but she bears more than a passing resemblance. Even taking in the fact she's been dead and buried a while."

"Please tell me she was in one piece?"

The hint of panic in Shona's voice seeped into Nina's brain. "Why?" Her voice was sharper than usual, especially when talking to the boss.

Shona explained what they'd found and whom they

thought it was.

"Just when you thought it couldn't get any worse." Abigail spoke for them all.

The walls of the briefing room now resembled a map of the London Underground, only with less order. The team, despite all the interviews hadn't come up with anything that would help them. There seemed to be no connection between any of the victims.

"Roy, do the deepest search you can on our victims and see what you can come up with."

He bounded off with a spring in his step. Roy, computers and the deep dark web were a ménage á trois that everyone celebrated.

"The rest of you get everything catalogued. I'll borrow Kelly and Brian again. They can go through the tapes looking for Barry."

"Kelly'll no' be happy, Ma'am."

"Kelly will just have to put on her big girl pants. She's a copper, not a ballerina."

They all stood up and shuffled off like they were about to be hanged by the neck until dead. Data entry being the most boring job on the planet it knocked their enthusiasm right out the window.

Shona contacted Cara's friend, Courtney and asked her to come in in the morning for another chat. She wasn't keen but Shona's threat of a squad car and handcuffs soon changed her mind. Hanging up the phone she rummaged in her drawer for a couple of paracetamol. There was a whole percussion section playing a tympani in her head. She snagged a coffee from the kitchen on her way to the office. Stewed and lukewarm it at least contained copious amounts of caffeine.

Roy didn't have much news for her and asked

permission to go into areas that were usually verboten.

"Go wherever you like."

"Excellent. I'll go to the Goosie Gander for a pint. Are you paying?"

"You'll be paying with your life if you don't find me something to hang our perverted serial killer."

In the only piece of reasonably good news, Mary rang to say that the torso had not been sexually abused.

"Thank heavens for that. If one can say it's a happy occasion a body has only been dissected."

"I hear you, Shona."

64

It turned out both Alexa and the BBC was right. The heavens opened that night and Shona awoke to a torrential downpour. Her drive to work seesawed between aquaplaning and driving through puddles so deep they could have their own name. Roads had turned into burns, as the Scots called streams. Shona was at the stage of understanding most Scottish words, and she particularly liked that one. It had a rather romantic overtone, like the Scottish bard himself.

Quietness reigned at the station with the team trickling in late. Abigail arrived first, closely followed by Roy. She agreed to help with Courtney's interview.

"Roy, have you anything for me yet?" She put her hand up face forward. "Before you answer if it's anything other than yes, you fired."

"I'll pack my desk up then, Ma'am."

"Get your head down and don't lift it until you give me a lead."

He was tapping furiously before she finished the sentence.

Courtney arrived at the appointed time. The whole team was present and correct, apart from Nina who appeared to be AWOL.

"She only lives in the Perth Road. She could walk here if the roads are impassable. Call her. Tell her to get her lazy backside here. Now."

Courtney hadn't improved any in the few days since they'd last met. She was still a sulky, snivelling, teenager. *Thank goodness most of the nurses up at the hospital aren't as bad as her. Please tell me she'll grow*

into a decent human being and a compassionate nurse?
Shona didn't think this would be the case. Not if her
present demeanour was anything to go by. She was
slouched down in the chair, arms folded and with a look
that any decent mother would slap off her face.

"How come you lot keep asking me here?"

"Because your friend is dead."

"I never did it."

"Shona rested her arms on the table and said in a
low voice, "Lose the attitude lady. I'm trying to solve a
murder. So sit up, smarten up and start answering
questions."

"Else what?" One side of her mouth shifted into a
sneer. She slouched further down in the chair.

"Else, I'll think you've something to hide,"
Shouted Shona. "Get rid of the freaking attitude." Her
voice rose higher still.

Courtney shot upright faster than shot from an
M134 minigun.

"You need to spill the beans about everything in
your friend's life, and I mean everything."

"There's nothing to tell." Her downcast eyes said
otherwise.

"You're hiding something."

"I'm not. Everybody loved Cara."

Shona slammed her hand on the table.

"Tell me the truth."

"I want a lawyer."

"What for, you're not under arrest."

"I'm entitled to one.

Shona phoned the duty lawyer who said he was about
ten minutes away. A visit to the office showed that
Nina was still missing in action. Or inaction if one
wanted to be entirely accurate.

"What's her excuse?"

Peter's worried look concerned Shona. A bomb could go off in the station and he would pick himself up off the floor and make a cup of tea.

"What's up?"

"She's not answering her phone, Ma'am."

"Nina? The original Little Miss Popular has her phone glued to her ear." Shona's heart beat a little faster and her pupils got a little larger. It would seem her fight or flight mechanism was alive and kicking in hard.

"Do her parents know where she is?"

"I haven't tried them. She's a grown woman. Felt a wee bittie odd." The anxious look did not sit well on the usually confident sergeant.

"I'll do it."

As she walked up the soulless corridor towards her office, Iain popped out of his room and asked if he could have a word.

"I'm a bit busy at the moment. Can't it wait?"

"I need to run something past you."

She followed him inside, pulled out a battered stool, and sat down.

"Shoot, but make it fast."

"There have been some strange anomalies in this case."

"And you think this is news? Someone dumping new bodies in old graves is the biggest anomaly of the lot."

"Yes, Ma'am. But there are more."

"Spit it out, Iain. We haven't got time for formality."

"There have been inordinate amounts of cigarette ends swept up as evidence."

"So far you're not lighting my fire, Iain. Graveyards are public places. Most people there are grieving. They're bound to have a fag."

"Yep, but not all of them are Optima."

"Is that mean to mean something to me?"

"This particular brand comes from Eastern Europe. Places like Poland and Russia."

"Russia. Are you saying The Alexeyevs are involved in this?"

"I'm not saying that. But they could be flogging illegally imported fags to our killer."

"Or they could be knee deep in the murders themselves."

"Not their style. Their victims would disappear for good."

"Anything else you've got for me."

"I'm a bit puzzled by the footprints."

"Which footprints."

"Forfar Old Churchyard Crypt."

"Oh, those ones?"

"The tread's not British and I'm having difficulty pinning them down."

"They're not Russian are they?"

"Not that I've found out so far. Not in the database."

"I need an answer soonest. Sooner even. Keep on it."

"Is everything okay, Ma'am." Shona's tone had his heart racing.

"Nina's missing."

Nina's mother was as puzzled as they were. "I thought she'd gone to work. Maybe, my girl she's not well. I'll check."

The phone went silent and Shona hung on, deep in thought.

"Her bed has not been slept in."

"Was she with Alejandro last night?"

"No. He is in Spain at a big dance competition."

Courtney had her lawyer present. Thankfully legal aid was beneath McLuskey and Runcie. This one was a spotty oink who turned out to be quite pleasant. He was also, much to Shona's surprise, quite sensible.

He stood when she entered the interview room and held out his hand. "Fraser Malcolm."

They'd no sooner sat down than he said, "My client would like to be completely honest with you."

"Yeh, right."

"I fully understand your scepticism, however, I have convinced her that full disclosure is in everyone's best interests."

Pleasant, sensible and long winded, thought Shona.

Courtney had moved from sullen to frightened in the space of twenty minutes.

"Courtney, I need to hurry you. More girls like Cara, or even you, could die."

The girl burst into tears.

Shona sighed, stood up and fetched a box of tissues from the side. She handed them to Courtney who pulled out a handful.

"Cara worked at Cat's Eyes."

Shona wasn't sure she'd heard correctly. Courtney's voice was muffled with tissues and sobs.

"Did you say Cat's Eyes?"

"Aye. As a barmaid."

"With the gear Cara was wearing, and her pearly whites, I'd say she was more than a barmaid," said Shona.

"Barmaid my backside. I know the barmaids at that place flash their tits, but they're not as young as the lap dancers."

"You've a delicate turn of phrase. How come you

know so much about this?"

"Trust me, you don't want to know."

"Seems to me that all roads in this case lead to that club. Ruskie 1 and 2 are so deep in this they'll never get out."

"I'd bet next months wages, you're right."

"Do you want a word with them?"

"Too right I do. Get them in here as fast as you can."

65

A thick, dark, cloak of desperation lay over the main office. No one could get hold of Nina, and it was now apparent she was a missing person. Shona briefed the chief who assured her any resources necessary would be instantly available. He said he would inform the chain of command and told her to get uniform involved in a search.

"Does anyone know what she was doing last night?" said Shona.

"She went clubbing. Asked the rest of us to go with her but we were too knackered," said Jason.

"I think she went to Peppermint Pink," added Abigail.

"Never heard of it. Where is it?"

"Down—"

"Actually never mind. Jason, Abigail, get down there. There will be a warrant waiting for you at the Sheriff's office. Get their CCTV images."

"What do you want us to do?" asked Peter.

"Roy, trace her phone then carry on with the searches I asked you to do."

Roy had already opened up his computer.

"Peter, go and take a statement from her parents."

"Saddest thing I'll ever have to do."

Shona bolted down to uniform and begged for extra personnel. Her oppo agreed she could have as many warm bodies as she required. She said to prepare them but she'd wait until the trace on Nina's phone came back. Hurrying back to her office she was intercepted by the duty sergeant. For once he looked more terrified than cheerful.

"Ma'am..." He stopped, swallowed and tried again. "Ma'am. They've found a body in Tayport Cemetery. All they'll say is that it's part of your case."

The world started to spin, went black and Shona smacked to the floor.

When she came to, Peter and the duty sergeant were staring at her. Peter fanned her with a copy of the courier, and the duty sergeant splashed water on her face.

"Give over the pair of you." She struggled up and leaned against the wall. "Give me that water." She chugged it down and asked Peter to find her something sweet.

She broke the news to the team that they were on their way to Tayport.

The journey was silent, the atmosphere sombre. Tension crackled between them and could have lit up the sky. Shona hesitated at the gate of the cemetery. Peter gently took her arm. She took a deep breath and walked through the gates.

This body was not in a grave but lying peacefully on top. Once again the death pose had been used.

At the sight of the body she sagged against him. He held her with a strong arm.

"It's not her, Shona. It's okay."

Shona sobbed as the relief swept over her. Then she felt guilty at being so pleased someone else was dead.

The woman was about Nina's age and so tanned so she almost looked Indian. However, her black hair showed about an inch of blonde at the roots Nothing like Nina's beautiful sheath of pure jet black.

"But who is she, and where does she fit into our

case?"

"We'll find that out, Ma'am. Dinnae you worry."

In their absence, Roy had managed to trace Nina's phone. It was somewhere near Tealing, a small village in Angus. . They jumped in cars and raced off. Secretly Shona didn't hold out any hope of finding Nina with it. Unless she was dead. No, don't let that be the case? Please? She could feel the blackness descending again and took some deep breaths. *Get a grip woman. You're an Inspector so act like one.* She thought things through. The likeliest scenario was that she'd been snatched. Whoever took her probably dumped her phone. Criminals were getting too damn smart. All those stupid telly programmes. This still didn't help them.

This proved to be the case, though not the part about the dead body. Not only had her phone been dumped, but her whole handbag and her shoes. The cherry red Jimmy Choo stilettos looked like blood against the dark green of the grass on which they lay. They were sodden through. *Nina will kill whoever did this to her pride and joy.*

Abigail's weeping could be heard for miles in the still air. Jason took four hurried steps and was sick. Even Peter looked like he could part with his lunch.

Shona forced herself to stay calm and take charge. "I know it's hard, but the best thing we can do for Nina is find her. If we fall apart that's not going to happen."

They regarded her with sad eyes.

Then Peter said, "You're right, Ma'am." He turned to the others and said. "Ma'am needs our help so pull yourselves together."

"If there's a positive note in any of this, it's this. At least we know where to start our search."

Their stares said Shona had to be kidding them.

The chief informed her the Chief Constable was on his way.

"He wanted to assure you that all personnel and resources of Police Scotland, are at your disposal."

"Thank you, Sir."

"What can I do to help?"

Even in the midst of this, Shona was taken aback.

"Nothing at the moment. The minute I need you I'll call."

At least I know in the midst of a disaster he can step up to the plate.

Nina woke in a bedroom she didn't recognise. She had the headache from Naraka, the Hindu equivalent of hell. The roiling in her stomach threatened to erupt and she thought she might actually be in hell. She looked around, taking stock of her surroundings.

Pink and orange wallpaper reminiscent of the sixties made her nausea even worse. The lurid orange carpet added to the queasiness. She forced herself to swallow. The room contained little furniture except the bed on which she lay. She was on top of a duvet with no cover. She pulled one hand. It moved about a foot and then stopped. The other hand the same. She was tied up. Feeling sick again she rolled over on to her side. She could do it if she kept her hands above her head. She shuffled to the edge of the bed, hung her head over and vomited. The effort almost pulled her arms out of their sockets. Forced to move back she swallowed rancid bile back down.

What the hell happened last night? She couldn't remember. Where was she? She vaguely remembered Peppermint Park. She pictured the packed dance floor and the vibrant thump of the music. Remembered going to the bar for a glass of wine. Then her mind went blank. A blinding flash. God, she'd been slipped a roofie. Had she been raped? No!

She froze as she heard the grating of a lock. What was going to happen to her? A figure appeared. Oh God, no.

Now she knew she really was in hell.

There were now more coppers squashed into the briefing room than was healthy. Every last one of them was champing at the bit to get going.

"Sgt Johnston is in charge. He will split you into three groups, which will be headed up by, Sgt Johnston, Sgt Lau and Sgt Bramwell."

One of the coppers put their hand up.

"Yes?"

"Sergeant Grant, Ma'am. Would you like me to head up a team as well? We might get further."

"Thank you, yes. Report to Sgt Johnston."

She hesitated before she said the next words. Tried to talk, and failed. Taking a deep breath she said, '"We are looking for Sgt Nina Chakrabarti." The next words she uttered tore her apart. Not only was Nina a colleague, but also one of her best friends. "I do not need to remind you that we may be looking for her body."

The grim faces staring at her reminded her of how well loved Nina was around the station. Some of the coppers including Abigail, were openly crying. Jason rubbed at his eyes but remained his usual tough ex squaddie self.

"The dog teams will meet you there."

The job would be near to impossible in this rain. *Why couldn't it have held off a few more days?*

Shona wished with every fibre of her being she could be with them. However, she knew she was needed here. Stopping the investigation was not even a remotely good idea. If Nina was still alive, the best way to find her was to find their killer. She watched the teams file out to the coaches that awaited them. For once there was no chatter. Just a weary, determined, silence in recognition of the ugly job ahead.

In her absence the chief had called a press briefing. Shona wasn't sure how she felt about this. It seemed too impersonal. The chief assured her it was necessary.

"We need every person in this city looking for her."

"Yes, Sir."

"How are you holding up?"

She stood taller. "I'm fine, Sir. That will be more than you can say about whoever has Nina, when I catch him."

"You may not want to issue threats in here." Considering the severity of what she had just said, the chief's tone remained calm.

"By the way," the chief continued. "I have had several complaints from Pa Broon."

"What about now? I've better things to worry me than that shyster's feelings."

"You are not doing enough to find his missing employee."

"First I've heard of it. Who?" This exchange was having the positive effect of making sure she was fired up and ready to shoot someone.

"A young man called Findlay Strachan."

"I'll be sure to look into it, Sir."

Her eyes said, the lad probably ran away from Mr Foul himself. His eyes gave nothing away.

"You do that, Shona."

With a considerably subdued team, Shona didn't know what to do with herself. She stomped into the office where Roy was hammering furiously at a keyboard.

"Anything yet?"

"Two of them worked for the council. Actually

three, if you count Tommy McShane who did a bit of cleaning there over a year ago. Lost his job in council cutbacks."

"I need more than that. I'm not convinced it's some demented member of the council who's doing this." A thought struck her like a billion volts of lightning. "Unless, of course, it's our esteemed Ex Lord Provost himself who's doing this."

"Pa Broon's mental and all, but he wouldn't cut off the cash cow. Tommy was a tenant."

"Who wasn't paying his bills."

"Not Broon's style."

Shona knew he was right. Brown's style was more torment them, chuck them out on the street or bend them to do your bidding.

A slow, painful hour passed with Shona doing very little. She asked Nina's parents to come to the station, assuring them it was not bad news. *Yet. I'm being so flexible with the truth here it's going to break.*

Nina's parents were stoic, understanding and appreciative of Shona's efforts.

"We know you will find our daughter," said her father.

"Of course you will. Nina always speaks highly of you. She wants to follow in your footsteps."

"She is strong and will not give up. We taught her to fight back. To bow to no one."

The use of the present tense broke Shona's heart into a million tiny pieces. Their hope and faith in her was almost too much too bear. She bit back tears and said, "We are doing everything to find her. We will keep you informed."

Shona phoned Peter who said, "Nothing yet, Ma'am.

Good or bad."

Nothing more needed to be said

Deep in her own grief, the opening of the door startled her. In walked Douglas.

"I heard you needed me."

She stood up and flew into his arms. They enveloped her and the dam broke.

The next interruption involved a silky coat and a warm tongue. Jock and Fagin had also heard she needed comfort.

68

Roy and Iain appeared at her door at the same time. They jostled to get through.

"Ma'am, you need to hear this," said Roy.

"I've got something for you." Iain's voice had urgency running right through it.

"Iain, you start." She ignored Roy's crestfallen expression. The wee sook would just have to suck it up.

"I've identified the make of shoe. It was a tough one but I got there. They're Russian."

The brothers Karamazov were definitely implicated in this. "How come it took so long to find this out?"

"They are hand made by one very exclusive firm in St Petersburg. So exclusive there is a waiting list to be accepted to buy them."

"Do thugs 1 and 2 wear them?"

"Their shoes do look pretty posh." Roy butted in. "Nina will…" His voice faded away.

Iain carried on."You know I was telling you about the cigarettes?"

"Half of Dundee smoke."

"I know, Ma'am, but we've got DNA on several of them that matches one person."

Shona's eyes lit up. "Please tell me it's one of the Alexeyevs."

"Gregor."

Shona shot out of her chair so fast she caused a fan effect.

Roy almost shouted. "That's what I wanted to tell you. Nadia Badowski is a distant cousin of the Alexeyevs."

"Let's go arrest him and find our Nina."

She phoned Sheriff Struthers. He assured her a warrant

would be waiting, no questions asked. She pleaded for more personnel from uniform. Three people would in no way be enough to arrest the Kalashnikov twins. The Inspector scrabbled around, found four willing volunteers, and handed them over without question. Given that one of the volunteers was Kelly, Shona had to question the veracity of the word willing. Unfortunately, Brian Gevers was already out searching for Nina.

Pistols were issued to everyone except Kelly. She, like the rest of them, wore a stab vest. Shona didn't like to think what Kelly would get up to with a pistol. Besides, she hadn't had the relevant training. Even the gun happy Shona wasn't stupid enough to put one in the hands of a rookie.

At midday Cat's Eyes held few punters. The ones ogling the performance wore suits. This indicated they'd nipped out in their lunch break for a wee bit of titillation. Shona scrutinised them, especially the position of their hands. *Yep. Titillation.*

Stephan wasn't his usual dour self. In fact he looked hellish. Someone had obviously stolen his caviar. The most interesting point of note was Gregor's absence.

"Where's your brother?"

"My brother's whereabouts has nothing to do with you."

"I'll think you'll find it does."

"Get out of my club or I will have you escorted from the premises. I do not take orders from women."

"What about women who have guns?"

Stephan found himself staring down the business end of a Glock 17. Far too close to his mouth for comfort, he decided it was easier to obey the inspector.

Especially when *she* decided it was time for a trip down to the station.

In a staccato gunfire of speech, Shona outlined all the evidence against Gregor. Shona filled his brother in on all the grisly details. Nothing left out. For good measure she added the names of the victims and what he had done to them.

"Now where is your brother?"

"I do not know. He is a free man."

"Every single piece of evidence leads to you and your club. Neither of you will be free men unless you spill the beans."

He was silent. His teeth clenched, a tic appeared at the corner of his mouth.

Shona slammed the file on the table. "Tell me where your brother is or I swear I will not be responsible for my actions."

Stephan glared at her.

Royally pissed off, Shona said, "Stephan Alexeyev, I am arresting you—"

Stephan's anger had reached the point of no return. "He has disrespected me. He has turned on our business, by killing our girls. He has broken the family code of honour."

Shona's eyes grew wide with shock. She didn't think any of this was actually going to work.

Stephan rattled off an address.

She informed him he would be kept under lock and key until his brother's arrest.

"Where on God's good earth is this?" She showed Roy the address.

"No clue, hang on." He pulled out his phone and tapped the screen a few times. "Deepest, darkest, out in the wilds, Angus."

69

They grabbed extra guns and a couple of squad cars. Shona took control of the wheel and they were soon screaming towards the house. Using hands free she phoned Peter.

"You and Abigail need to meet us at..." She rattled off the address. "Explanation later but it possibly involves Nina."

She hung up. The mention of Nina would lend wings to their wheels.

Jason spent the entire journey moaning about Shona's driving.

Shona's nerves, sensitive at the best of times, were now shot to pieces.

"Shut up and stop whining. You can be a real wuss at times."

They all arrived together.

"We think Nina may be holed up in there." She didn't mention the fact she was sending up urgent prayers her sergeant was alive. She swallowed down the tears. The Victorian mansion was built from local stone. Usually beautiful beige, the relentless rain dulled it to dark grey bleakness. As they approached a gunshot was heard.

"Move, now." Shona's voice left no room for argument.

They all ran towards the front door rather than cover, testament to their need to find their missing colleague.

"Jason, round the back." Her voice was urgent, yet low. No use alerting Gregor to their movements.

Peter whispered in her ear. "He could kill anyone in the house."

"I know." She shouted. "Let's move."

In a twinkling of an eye a battering ram was put to good use and the front door swung open.

"Fan out. Be careful."

The house was eerily quiet. More ominously, the gunfire had stopped. They crept forward, every step cautious. They were not dealing with your average low life that turned to a life of crime. Russian Mafia, Gregor learned law breaking as he suckled on his mother's breast.

As they approached doors they were opened, guns at the ready. All empty.

"Upstairs."

The first door they came to was locked. No key. "Battering ram. Now." Her voice, no longer quiet, echoed around the vast hallway.

A terrified girl lay in the room, Emaciated and filthy, her blonde hair matted, she didn't move. Shona ran to the bed and felt her pulse. Thready but definitely there. "Can you hear me?" There was no movement. Shona took a deep breath and said to Peter, "You are a witness that I'm doing this for her own good."

She lightly slapped the girl's face. "Come on. Waken up. It's the police. We're here to help you."

The girl moaned and her eyelids fluttered. Shona reassured her. "Everything is going to be okay." A stray tear slid down the lassie's face and soaked into the uncovered duvet.

"We'll be back soon. You're safe."

They raced from the room. The scenario was repeated in another five rooms. All occupied, but in various stages of deprivation.

They battered down the last door and Shona

collapsed against the frame. The room contained Nina, tied to the bed and looking like she'd been chewed by an elephant and spat out again, but alive. Apparently she was also her usual cheeky self. "You took your time."

"You're late for work." Shona hurried over and stepped in a pool of vomit. Paying it no heed she hugged Nina like she'd been gone for a thousand years.

"I take it you've missed me?"

Deciding Nina was up to some work, Shona said, "Enough of the loafing about. You're in charge here. There are several other rooms with people in. Sort them out." She chucked her phone at Nina. "In case you need us. Phone for ambulances."

She ran from the room leaving Nina behind.

All bravado gone, tears rolled down Nina's face.

"Ma'am, down here." Roy stood beside an open door. They dashed down and found themselves in some sort of war room. Photos, maps, lists and diagrams covered the walls. They noticed the open door just as the roar of an engine started.

"Move!"

A Lamborghini screeched down the driveway.

Tumbling into squad cars they set off in hot pursuit, blue lights flashing and sirens blazing. Much as she wanted to catch Gregor, Shona had to use a light foot on the pedal. Torrential rain, after a long dry spell, meant treacherous driving conditions.

"He cannae' go that fast in this. No' on these roads."

"Do you think Gregor's worrying about that?" said Shona.

Ma'am—"

"For heavens sake, Jason, will you shut it? Do you want to catch Nina's abductor?"

"Of course. I'd like to be in once piece while we do it."

"Wee sleekit, cowran, timorous beastie, O' what a panic's in the breastie!"

"Ha flaming Ha. I'm terrified here."

If Shona was perfectly honest, it was the jokes that were getting her through this.

"I'll be sure to bring a tank next time. You might feel a wee bit braver then."

Startled by the commotion, horses, sheep and cattle scattered. Roy, hanging out of the window, could just about see the Lamborghini in the distance. Water dripped down his face and neck before escaping under his shirt. "Next left. Tight turn."

Shona screeched round the corner, tires smoking. Jason gripped the edge of the seat so hard his finger went through the fabric.

"Right in about a hundred yards."

"Shona followed his directions. Roy was whooping and holding on tight to the top of the car. "This is amazing."

"You're easy pleased, laddie, and in a dangerous position"

"He's right, get back in here and buckle up."

Roy obeyed. "I was enjoying that." He wiped his wet face with the edge of his shirt.

Shona slowed to take a sharp bend. It was a good job she did. Gregor hadn't been quite so careful and the Lamborghini was now wrapped around a tree. Smoke poured from the engine. They jumped from the squad car and raced towards Gregor. He was conscious but moaning. Flames licked at the edges of the Lamborghini.

"Get him out."

They dragged him well back from the car,

moments before it exploded.

Shona sank onto the wet grass, then pulled herself together. "Gregor Alexeyev. I am arresting you for the murders of…"

70

Five hours later Shona sat in her office, dirty and exhausted. Gregor had not said one word since his arrest, and was under guard in Ninewells Hospital.

They had no clue as to his motives and might never find out. Stephan refused to visit his brother. McLuskey and could not represent him, as she was too close to the case. He was truly alone.

Nina and the other occupants of the mansion had all been checked out in A&E. Most were kept in, but she was discharged and insisted she return to work.

Shona was sipping cold coffee and attempting to muster up the energy to update HOLMES when the door opened. Douglas walked in.
"I thought you might like company."
"That would be awesome, but it's going to be hours before I get to leave."
"I thought that might be the case." He pulled a small box from his pocket. "I was waiting for the perfect time, but that will never happen with you." He got down on one knee and opened the box to expose a sparkling diamond. "Shona McKenzie, will you marry me?"
Cheers erupted from the team, who were in on the secret. Nina cheered the loudest of all. The tilt to her world disappeared and life returned to normal.
"Your timing sucks, but the answer is Yes."

WENDY H. JONES

Wendy H. Jones lives in Dundee, Scotland, and her police procedural series featuring Detective Inspector Shona McKenzie, is set in Dundee.

Wendy, who is a committed Christian, has led a varied and adventurous life. Her love for adventure led to her joining the Royal Navy to undertake nurse training. After six years in the Navy she joined the Army where she served as an officer for a further 17 years. This took her all over the world including the Middle East and the Far East. Much of her spare time is now spent travelling around the UK, and lands much further afield.

As well as nursing Wendy also worked for many years in Academia. This led to publication in academic textbooks and journals. Killer's Crew is the fifth book in the Shona McKenzie series.

THE DI SHONA McKENZIE MYSTERIES

Killer's Countdown
Killer's Craft
Killer's Cross
Killer's Cut
Killer's Crew

FERGUS AND FLORA MYSTERIES

The Dagger's Curse

FIND OUT MORE

Website: http://www.wendyhjones.com

Full list of links: http://about.me/WendyHJones

Twitter: https://twitter.com/WendyHJones

Photographs of the places mentioned in the book can be found at: http://www.pinterest.com/wjones64/my-dundee/

Lightning Source UK Ltd.
Milton Keynes UK
UKOW04f1930090817
307021UK00001B/3/P